LIVE BY THE GUN

Bud Tilden wanted to make a life farming. But when he walked into an ambush of Comanche's Deputy—and killed one of the attackers—the whole town called him a hero. Before he knew it, Bud had killed again, and again, and then again. Outlaws soon came looking for him.

But somewhere deep inside, Bud knew it had to stop. And somewhere in the shadows of Comanche, a killer was waiting for Bud to put down his gun . . .

Also available from Gunsmoke

Mattie by Judy Alter
Ride Down the Wind by Wayne Barton
Tragedy Trail by Max Brand
Black Hats by David Case
The Fighting Breed by David Case
The Night Branders by Walt Coburn
Flame in the Forest by Al Cody
Return to Texas by Al Cody
Gold Train by Jess Cody
Slaughter at Buffalo Creek by Chet Cunningham
Broken Creek by Lee Floren
The Rawhide Men by Lee Floren
Full Circle by Stephen E. Fugate
Death Ground by Edward Gorman
Lassiter Tough by Loren Zane Grey
Lassiter and The Great Horse Race by Loren Zane Grey
Lassiter on the Texas Trail by Loren Zane Grey
Lassiter's Ride by Loren Zane Grey
Forlorn River by Zane Grey
Border Legion by Zane Grey
The Man of the Forest by Zane Grey
The Spirit of the Border by Zane Grey
Thunder Mountain by Zane Grey
Wyoming by Zane Grey
Duel at Gold Buttes by William Jeffrey
The Hangman by Justin Ladd
The Half-Breed by Justin Ladd
The Pursuers by Justin Ladd
The Sharpshooters by Justin Ladd
Gunplay Over Laredo by Norman A. Lazenby
Wild Horse Shorty by Nelson Nye
Cartridge Case Law by Nelson Nye
Gunman, Gunman by Nelson Nye
Rafe by Nelson Nye
Break the Young Land by T. V. Olsen
A Killer is Waiting by T. V. Olsen
Savage Sierra by T. V. Olsen
The Stalking Moon by T. V. Olsen
The Carnady Feud by Dean Owen
Crusade on The Chisholm by Roe Richmond
The Man From Tombstone and Gunfight at Ringo Junction by Jack Slade
Ballanger by Robert E. Trevathan

LIVE BY THE GUN

Wayne Barton
and Stan Williams

GUNSMOKE

WESTERNS

First published 1989
by Pocket Books

This hardback edition 1990
by Chivers Press
by arrangement with
Pocket Books
A Division of Simon & Schuster, Inc

ISBN 0 86220 966 8

British Library Cataloguing in Publication Data

Barton, Wayne
Live by the gun.
I. Title II. Williams, Stan
813.54 [F]

ISBN 0–86220–966–8

This novel is a work of fiction. Names, characters, places and incidents are either the product of the author's imagination or are used fictitiously. Any resemblance to actual events or locales or persons, living or dead, is entirely coincidental.

Printed and bound in Great Britain by
Redwood Press Limited, Melksham, Wiltshire

Live By The Gun

Chapter 1

I'D SLUNG THE HANG ROPE over an oak limb and was just about to hoist my buck by his antlers when I saw the rider coming in. At first he wasn't more than a tall shadow against the sunset, so I didn't pay him much mind. A lot of folks stopped to camp at the Wells. It wasn't too usual for a lone man to ride in so late, but it wasn't anything uncommon either. After all, I was there alone.

That was a little different. I was on a hunting trip, just a few miles from home. The rest of the campers looked like families traveling, mostly—that and a crew of Mexican cedar cutters and a few out-of-work cowhands passing through. They were there for the same reason as me, the good water at the Wells. Fact is, I hadn't paid any of them much mind either. It had been a long time since lunch, and not much of that, so I was about ready to eat and turn in.

The rider had already passed the first couple of places he might have stopped. I glanced at him again, then put my back into hauling the buck snug up against the limb and safe from coyotes. November nights are cold in central Texas, so I figured the meat would chill out by morning. Feeling good, I went to my wagon to check the grub box. I'd put coffee on to boil before I started with the deer. Now sundown was so near that I'd have to cook in the dark or get by on an airtight of peaches and some of yesterday's hard biscuits. I'd about decided on the peaches when I heard a horse pull up right behind me. The lone rider spoke in a voice I'd known all my life.

"Well, look-a-here. First night out from home, and I find me a real desperado."

"Davy! I wouldn't have thought about you for a dollar!"

Davy Johnson was leaning on his saddle horn, grinning down at me. He had his hat off, and his thatch of blond hair looked like somebody's hayrick. He was bundled in the big sheepskin coat he always wore on the trail. His deputy's star was pinned over the left pocket. He was twenty-two, two years older than me, and I'd tagged after him ever since we'd been big enough to walk. Now he had him a pretty wife and a year-old daughter and a county job that had brought him to my campfire.

"Maybe I'll come in peaceable," I told him. "Do you feed your prisoners good?"

He laughed softly. "Shoot, Bud, the county can't afford to feed you. It'd pay me to hang you right away." He nodded toward the deer. "Probably I ought to confiscate that buck. What is he, seven points?"

"Six." He didn't make any move to get down, so I added, "What brings you out here, some kind of lawman business?"

"Sort of. Old Sam Reynolds, he thinks some of his calves might have had a little help straying off and getting lost. I'm out seeing who we have traveling through." He grinned at me. "I've already talked to your neighbors. That little Johnnie MacNally's growing up real pretty. If she was my neighbor, I'd see if I couldn't scrub her down a little and get her into a dress."

"Nothing to do with me," I said. "Why did you stop out there?"

He shrugged. "Like always. Any time there's trouble we think about the MacNallys first. They've quieted down a little since Mark got married, though."

There were four of the MacNallys, Matthew, Mark, Luke, and young Johnnie. Their ma had been a determined woman, and she hadn't varied from her plan for naming them just because the last one had betrayed her by being a girl. They all lived out on the spread just west of my farm. Gossip said their pa had gotten his start by selling other folks' cattle in Mexico, and most people didn't figure his sons were too different. They were good neighbors, though—most of the time.

"Luke's still wild enough," I said.

Davy laughed. "Guess you wouldn't mind seeing me put Luke away for ten or twenty years." His voice turned serious. "Is he still holding a grudge over you and Annette?"

"I reckon so." Luke MacNally was the same age as me. We hadn't ever gotten along any too well, especially not after we both got sweet on Annette Stanton. I was figuring on marrying her. "Luke's not the forgiving kind."

"You look out for him. He'd like to prove he's as hard a man as those brothers of his."

"Nothing to do with me." I turned away to see to the coffeepot. I didn't want to talk about Luke. "Why don't you light down from that nag and have some coffee? I'm getting a crick in my neck looking at you."

Davy shook his head, letting his eyes play over the campsites, seeing all he could before the dark came down completely. He kept coming back to the next campfire down from mine, maybe fifty yards away. One man was squatting against the base of a big oak with his head down across his folded arms. His partner was up chopping more firewood, the strokes of his ax singing up toward us hard and sharp just a second after the blade cut wood.

"You know anything about those fellers?" Davy asked suddenly.

I shook my head. "Haven't spoken to them. There's a bunch of Mennonites on down the way. They might be more your speed if you're looking for somebody to pick on."

"Aw, if I wanted easy pickings, I'd go after you. Probably have to tie one of my hands, so's to make it interesting." He glanced toward the other fire again, then back at me. "Reckon you'll have room for me to bed down here?"

"Sure, and venison tenderloin for supper. Been a long time since we shared a campfire. I'm surprised Sheriff Stanton could pry you away from Alene and little Beth for a night."

Davy shrugged, but I could see his face go wistful. "Part of the job." He rubbed at the blond stubble on his chin. "Sure beats following a mule around the farm. Come right down to it, there ain't much that's less interesting than the hind end of a mule."

"Farming's not so bad. Once in a while farmers even do something else. Like now I'm out hunting, just the way you and me used to do."

Probably I sounded a little sharper than I meant to, because Davy moved to look at me. "No offense, Bud," he said. "Fact is, I don't think about you as a farmer."

"That's what I am."

"Maybe not for always." He rubbed his chin again. "I been meaning to talk to you, Bud," he said. "I'm thinking Sheriff Stanton may not run for another term. Might be I could take his place—and I'd be wanting a good deputy."

It was my turn to laugh. "You mean me? I'm not any gunman."

"A gunman's not what I'd be looking for." Davy's voice got serious again. He leaned forward, and the polished brass of his badge gleamed in the firelight. "The county's changing, Bud. There's a lot of new families moving into Comanche now that the railroad's come. I'd need a man that cares about people . . ."

He broke off. Down at the next camp the sound of the ax had stopped. The second man was standing motionless, looking our way. He was at the edge of the firelight, and I had a glimpse of deep-set eyes, a sharp nose, teeth flashing in a tangled beard. His partner still leaned against the tree. He had his head up now, his face turned our way but hidden by the dancing shadows.

Davy straightened in his saddle, and his big bay horse gave a little prancing step as if he knew something was coming up.

". . . the way you do," Davy finished. "Listen, Bud, I'd better go have a word with those two. I'll be back directly for a plate of beans. We can talk more then."

"I'll have the coffee boiling," I said. "You haven't said a word about Beth or Alene."

"That Beth!" He laughed. "Smartest kid I ever saw. Wait'll I tell you."

He rode on down the trail that hooked up all the camping grounds, and the man waiting there stepped out to meet him. I turned back to the chuck box on my wagon. The idea of cooking sounded a lot better now; it makes a real difference when there's a friend to share the meal. I dug down to get a can of beans, which is why I didn't see what happened next.

There must have been some talk, too quiet for me to hear even if I'd been paying attention. I heard the scream, though. It was a man's voice, hoarse and ringing. A woman's scream can mean anything; a man doesn't scream any more often than a horse, nor for any less reason. I came out of that wagon fast. To this day I don't remember drawing it from its boot, but my old Winchester was in my hands when I hit the ground. Next I knew, I was levering a shell into its chamber and looking hard to see where the sound had come from. The whole place had gone quiet as a church.

It was that time just ahead of night when the sky still shows blue, just shading into greens and grays. A few clouds down low in the west were shining like melted brass. Below the sky's glow all I saw was shadows moving down by the camp where Davy had gone. Then the bay horse reared and danced backward on its hind legs, and the shadows turned into Davy and the horse and the drifter with the ax.

Davy had lost his hat. He was leaning in the saddle, reaching for his pistol, I thought. The drifter was on him like a border collie herding sheep, rushing right up almost under the horse's belly. Before I could understand what he meant to do he'd drawn back and chopped the ax blade into the bay's ribs with a solid, biting *thunk*.

"Hey!" I yelled, but nobody heard me. The horse screamed and bucked. The saddle came off, taking Davy with it. The big bay horse broke into the darkness on a dead run. The drifter lunged at Davy like a striking rattler. Firelight glinted on the blade of the ax, and then the muzzle flash of my carbine blinded me for a second so I couldn't see what was happening.

I don't remember aiming, and I sure didn't know I was going to shoot. It just happened. Even so, the bullet must have come somewhere close, because the one with the ax dropped it and straightened up, turning my way. I'd sort of lost track of his partner until another muzzle flash blossomed over to my left, this one smaller and aimed my way. A bullet whined off something behind me, and I snapped a shot his way without really noticing him. He stumbled backward against the tree like he'd tripped over one of its roots, but I didn't care about him. My mind could still see that ax swinging toward Davy, and my eye was on the man who'd held it.

He was lifting a handgun in my direction when I fired the third time. That bullet took him solidly enough to stagger him backward. The next one knocked him down. He fell into the fire, and I shot him again. Walking down the slope toward him, I put another bullet into his smoldering vest. He didn't even jerk, but I kept shooting until there was no more muzzle flash, just the snap of the hammer against the firing pin.

Maybe that was what brought me back to my senses. Leaving the drifter where he'd fallen, I dropped the rifle and stumbled over to Davy. He way lying by his saddle, all crumpled up. My first thought was that one of his legs was a lot longer than the other. It only looked that way. The ax had cut through the saddle girth. Before that it had gone through Davy's leg and the stirrup strap. The only time I'd ever seen so much blood was once when Pa killed a hog—with an ax.

"Davy," I said, real soft, like I was afraid of waking him. I leaned close, and that was when I saw his right hand and his pistol were missing.

By that time the camp was in a real hooraw. Likely everybody had gone ducking for cover at the first shot, but now they'd dragged out their artillery and were running to see where the war was. They all must have been yelling at once, but underneath the noise came a hoarse whisper.

"Bud."

It wasn't any voice I'd ever heard before. Davy was looking at me. In the firelight his face was chalky white, and his blue eyes had a puzzled expression. His lips moved again.

"Little Beth." His voice was thin as woodsmoke. "Smartest kid I've ever . . ." Then the light died out of his eyes like a lamp when the last little bit of oil burns away. I'd never had a better friend nor ever would.

Next thing I knew, somebody was poking me in the ribs. I realized that had been going on for a minute or so before I turned around. A heavyset man with a grizzled brown beard was nudging at me with the barrels of a shotgun.

"On your feet, you murderin'—" he was saying, but I wasn't in any mood to pay attention. I came up fast, twisting the gun away from him—I don't know why it didn't go off—and chucking it toward the fire. Two of the Mennonite men were trying to keep Davy's killer from burning, and they scattered pretty fast when the shotgun lit beside them. I turned my back on the whole bunch while I slipped off my jacket and laid it over Davy's face.

Which was when three of the cedar choppers grabbed me by the arms from behind and hustled me back toward the fire. I guess I tried to make a fight of it. I was a head taller than any of them, so at first I shook them around pretty good. All of a sudden, though, I went weak as a newborn colt. Everything turned sort of hazy, and I'd have fallen if they hadn't been holding me up.

One of the cedar crew held out a coil of rope and spoke in Spanish. The words didn't register, but I knew what he meant, all right; it just didn't seem important right then. The Mennonites had rolled the killer out of the fire. They were pouring water on his clothes, looking up at me every now and then like I was a rabid wolf somebody had just brought in. Grizzled Beard had his shotgun back. He came up in front of me and jammed the muzzle into my stomach.

"Now, mister, I guess we'll just take care of you."

I looked at him, where he was standing, and everything was clear again. "God damn you," I said.

Probably I still wasn't myself, because I'd never spoken like that to a living soul before. It caught him by surprise, too, and then I did start to fight.

"Damn you!" I yelled again. "Get off his hand!"

When the grizzled man saw it—Davy's hand still clutching the pistol—under his boot, he reeled backward, looking sick. The man with the rope whispered, *"Madre de Dios."* He seemed a few years older than the others, with a dark, thin face and a heavy gray mustache. He came up close and stared into my eyes.

"Mi amigo," I said, nodding toward Davy's body. The older of the Mennonites went over and knelt there, pulling back the jacket to look. The first thing he saw was Davy's badge.

"Wait," he said in a heavy German accent. "This one a lawman is. What has happened here?"

I did my best to explain, though I'm still not sure just what I said. Whatever it was, it was enough to change everybody's mind about hanging me. They kept asking questions about it until finally a sleepy-looking old man came wagging a wooden water barrel up from the lower camp.

"What I want to know is who's going to pay for this." He held it up without even a glance at the two dead men. A last mouthful of water slopped out of a splintered hole toward the bottom of the barrel. "It's plumb ruined, and maybe two days to the next good water."

I remembered my first wild shot and figured I was probably to blame. "Take mine," I told him. "I'm not far from home."

Saying that, it came to me that I'd never felt any farther from home. Davy was dead, and I was just starting to realize I'd killed a man—shot him to pieces. Pa had always taught it was sinful to take a human life, whatever the reason, and now I'd done it. I wasn't even sure whether I was trying to save Davy's life, or if I'd just been bent on killing the man who'd hurt him.

At least, I told myself, that part was over. I would bury my old deer rifle out behind the barn and never shed the blood of any living thing again. That would make an end of it—over and done with.

"*Amigo,* here." It was the cedar chopper who'd wanted to hang me. He held out a half-empty whiskey bottle. "Drink," he said when I hesitated. "You feel better."

I had my doubts, but I took a swallow and choked. The stuff burned all the way down, and I had some idea why Pa had always been so set against it. But I did feel better.

"*Gracias, amigo,*" I said, handing it back. He nodded seriously.

"The sheriff comes soon. You come to our camp, wait with us, *que?*"

"Thanks."

I started to follow him, but just then the youngest of the Mennonite men came up to us.

"Friend," he said, "there is blood on the tree."

The cedar cutter looked at me. I frowned and tried to make sense of his words, but all I could think of was Calvary's tree in the old hymns.

"I'm sorry," I said. "Meaning no disrespect, but I don't understand your ways."

Now he looked puzzled, but he shook his head. "No, over here." He pointed toward the big oak where I'd first seen the drifters camped. "I think the other man must have been wounded. He rode away while you were still shooting."

Chapter 2

MA HAD A STACK of wheat cakes waiting in the warming cupboard above the cookstove when Pa and I got home. She brought them down, then set out a platter of sausage and soft-fried eggs while we were still taking off our coats. I don't expect I ever looked at a better breakfast, nor ever enjoyed one any less.

It wasn't quite daybreak. I was bone-tired, like I'd been plowing all night long. I'd told what had happened two or three more times, then brought Davy into town in my wagon. Folks at the Wells had figured to put the man I'd shot in with him. I wouldn't have it, so that probably cost us another hour. The sky had just been going to blues and grays—this time in the east—when I'd finally braked in front of Perry's Hardware and Woodworks, which was also Comanche's funeral parlor. Sheriff Stanton stepped down from his big black road horse and motioned to me.

"Here, Bud, you come along to the office. These

other folks can take care of things. I still got a few questions I need to ask."

I nodded dumbly to the men waiting in the cold—it was Mr. Perry and Alf Cryer, his helper—then went along with the sheriff. I figured he just wanted to keep me from having to see them carry Davy inside, but by now I had a question of my own.

"Why would a man do something like that? And to Davy? I don't think Davy even knew who he was."

Sheriff Stanton turned from hanging up his long duster coat and looked at me. He was drooping like his thick silver mustache, seeming six inches shorter than the last time I'd seen him.

"Might be we'll find the reason in here, Bud." He sank down into his office chair and dropped a hand on the pile of handbills on the desk. "You saw that feller about as well as anybody. Take a look."

I didn't have to look far. He was about halfway down. His hair and beard were trimmed a little neater in the picture, but it was the man who'd killed Davy. Sheriff Stanton must have seen the answer in my face.

"Trey Bonner," he read, squinting at the poster. "Wanted for robbery and murder." He shook his head. "Poor Davy. He just happened onto him without knowing no better."

Looking at the sheriff, I remembered something Davy had told me earlier that night. Now I saw he'd been right; Amos Stanton didn't look like he wanted to run for office again.

About that time was when Pa showed up. He and Ma had moved into town nearly a year back, with me staying on to work the farm. Losing half a night's sleep hadn't made Pa look any younger either. He put his stout arm around me, gave me an awkward hug, and asked if I'd finished flat-breaking the fields before I went hunting.

I had, but I don't guess I ever answered. Instead, I told him about the deer. That six-pointer was as fine a buck as I'd ever brought down, and I'd left him for the camp at the Wells. Pa never said a word about the killings, and it came to me that he was a kind man. That's the sort of day it turned out to be—a day when I saw deep enough to understand things somebody smarter might have known with just a glance.

Anyway, I sat at the kitchen table with my head hanging and my hands wrapped tight around my coffee mug. Finally I said, "I've done what you've always taught me was wrong. I've gone and killed a man."

It hadn't really sunk in until I heard myself say it. Then I had to go right quick and wash my face. I hadn't cried since I was twelve years old, but I sure recognized the signs. After that I managed to tell pretty much what had happened, right up to the end.

"I declare, I can't see how you could just up and forget that other man who'd tried to shoot you," Ma was saying, when there came the first knock at the door. It was the preacher, Brother Winslow.

"I'm sorry to come calling so early," he said. "I thought I should just stop by. It's really on my way home."

Brother Winslow took a cup of coffee and a seat in the kitchen. He had his burying face on that morning. He was still a youngish man, but he seemed always to have a lot on his mind. I'd never understood why, since he didn't have to work or fret about crops.

"Did you say you hadn't been home?" Ma asked him.

"No, I'm afraid I haven't." He took a deep swallow from his cup. "Wonderful coffee, Mrs. Tilden, as always. No, Mrs. Winslow and I have been sitting up with poor Alene Johnson. She's taken Davy's death pretty hard."

"I guess you were the one had to tell her, Preacher?" Pa asked.

Brother Winslow looked up with a quick, gray nod. "Yes. What little I knew. These eggs are just the thing to start the day on." He turned his tired eyes on me. "It's Bud she wants to speak to, though."

My stomach turned over and drew up into a ball, like an armadillo trying to protect itself. I'd been working hard not to remember about Davy's wife. Now I knew I'd have to talk to Alene before I slept again. That seemed harder than anything else I'd done that night, and maybe I started to understand why things seemed to ride so heavy on Brother Winslow. He finished his coffee, answered the door at the next knock, and slipped away without my noticing.

He'd let in the widow Mabry, Ma's closest neighbor. "Ruth, Henry, good morning." She plunked down a loaf wrapped in cloth on the table. "I've brought you all some raisin cake." Then she turned to me. "I know it's early, but I just had to come over and give you a big hug, Bud Tilden."

She did, too. She was a tall, strong woman, smelling of lilac powder and soap and fresh raisin cake with a touch of rum in it.

"Henry Tilden, Jr.," she said, stepping back to arm's length but still hanging onto me. "We're all just so *proud* of you! Ain't you the perfect son, though—tall like your mama and stout like your daddy."

I muttered a thank you without having the least idea what she was talking about, and then Ma took over and got Widow Mabry settled with a cup of coffee. If Gabriel came around blowing the last trumpet, Ma wouldn't think of going with him until he'd come in for coffee.

No, Widow Mabry wouldn't eat with us. Well, maybe just one of those wheat cakes. Land's sake, a body didn't know what to think, with all the new people coming into the county and so much meanness going on. She just had to hear what had happened at the Wells from my own lips.

I got up from the table for no special reason, just for something to do. Being up, I went to look out the window. Pa was talking quietly to the widow, and she was all sympathy. I parted the window curtains and rested my head against the smooth wood of the frame.

Out in the drive a plump, plain lady was getting out of her little side-spring buggy. She had an old flatiron on a leather strap, and she hooked it to the horse's rigging to keep him hitched there. Then she bent to set it right between his forefeet, because Julia Stanton was too careful a woman just to drop it.

I saw all that, but most of my attention was on her daughter. Annette Stanton stepped down as delicately as a doe coming to drink, her head up with that same listening wariness. She was the first person all morning I'd been pleased to see.

"Bud?" Ma called. "Who's there?"

"It's just Mrs. Stanton."

"Did Sheriff Stanton come with her?"

"No, it's Annette with her. And Will."

Widow Mabry clucked in her throat. "Our little Annie is growing up," she said. If she was saying it for my benefit, she was wasting words. I knew probably better than anybody how much Annette had grown up.

I answered the door. Mrs. Stanton patted me on the shoulder and smiled. For the first time I noticed how pretty she was, in a motherly sort of way. It made me think what a beauty she must have been at Annette's age. That got my mind back on Annette, and I came to meet her at the door.

A head shorter than me, Ann stood with the first

sunlight turning her hair the color of new cornsilk. I'd never been sure what color her eyes were. Today they looked pale brown with little flecks as green as a new leaf, so soft and shy that I thought of the doe again. She took a step like she might hug me the way the widow had, but then Will shoved between us. He was carrying a big covered platter.

"Gosh, Bud, did you really shoot that man? Was he an outlaw, like Pa said? Where can I put this down?"

Will was barely fourteen, a skinny, towheaded kid who seemed always in the way when I wanted to be alone with Annette. Likely he felt pretty much the same about me. His mother collared him before I had to think of an answer.

"You take that right to the sideboard, young man, and don't bother Bud." Her voice was soft, more southern than western. "I doubt he feels much like talking just now."

Then Ma bustled up with fresh cups. We all started for the kitchen table, but then Ma said we should move to the parlor. We'd just settled there when somebody else knocked on the door. This time Pa went to answer, and I ended up on the sofa between Ann and her mother, with Will squeezed in, too, and looking up at me like I was something brand new. Ann lifted her head to whisper in my ear, "Bud, I'm so proud I could just kiss you!"

That seemed like a fine idea, but not right then. I can't remember who arrived next, but by seven o'clock the house was full of people bringing dishes of food just like somebody had died—somebody in the family, I mean. They all wanted to know what had happened, but Widow Mabry headed them off.

"You all let Bud be, now. He's just too modest for his own good."

" 'Scuse me," I said, and I sidled off to answer the

door. Somebody else could have done it, but I needed to get away. Most likely I was still thinking about what the widow had said, because I wasn't expecting who I met in the doorway.

Standing there was one of the prettiest girls I'd ever seen—so pretty, in a lonely sort of way, that for a minute I didn't know who she was. Raven-black hair framed her small, triangular face and dropped free to her shoulders. A blue gingham dress clung to her body like a child to its mother until it came to her waist, then flowed down and out in soft pleats. My eyes followed that blue flow all the way to her shoes. I was beginning to wish I knew her when she said, "Bud?"

When she spoke, I did know her. "Hello, Johnnie," I said. "You look different."

"It's the dress," she said. There was some embarrassment in her voice, because I was still staring. "It's new, from material I ordered."

That was partly true. I'd probably never seen Johnnie MacNally in a dress before. I remembered Davy had mentioned how she would look, and I could see he'd been right.

"Come in."

"Oh, no." Johnnie held out a dish. "I'll just leave this. I—we—all of us wanted to say how sorry we were about what happened, that's all. I'll be thinking about you today."

I started to say there was no need, because nothing had happened to me. Then Ma came up to see why I was letting the cold air in.

"Why, Johnnie! You haven't been to visit since we moved into town. You just put that dish in the kitchen and have some coffee with us."

"No, thank you, Mrs. Tilden. I don't drink coffee."

Johnnie might as well have tried to say no to a four-horse team. Ma took her into the kitchen. In a minute they came back, Johnnie holding a glass of fresh buttermilk in place of a cup. I'd mostly seen her in clothes her brothers had cast off, and that blue dress made a real difference. I was still noticing that when Annette came over and took my arm.

"Bud, I know Alene Johnson wanted to see you. Mama says everybody will be taking things over there soon. Maybe we should go on ahead."

Johnnie had stopped by Ma's old piano. She looked at Ann, then at me.

"Well, sure." I said. Whatever I'd been thinking, Ann's words brought back the fact of Davy's death. "I guess we'd better."

It took a minute to get loose from those folks in the parlor, and another minute for Ann to convince Will he wasn't going with us. I'd meant to thank Johnnie for coming, but she was already talking to the widow, her back turned to us as we left.

Ann gave me that kiss she'd promised as soon as we were in the buggy. I reached to put my arm around her, but she scooted away against the far side of the seat.

"Well, Bud Tilden, I didn't know you were so friendly with your neighbors!"

"I guess so. They all meant well, coming by like that."

"You know very well who I mean! Why did *she* come to your house? The MacNallys don't even come to church."

I've already said the MacNally boys didn't have any too good a reputation in town. It didn't seem right to take that feeling out on Johnnie, though.

"It's Pa's house, not mine," I said. "And the church isn't their denomination."

"Oh? Just what *is* their denomination, then?"

I didn't know. The old MacNallys were dead and

gone. They must have been *something,* else they wouldn't have named their children the way they had. I didn't say any more, though, because we were pulling up in front of the last little house on the east lane. I gave Ann my hand to help her down. She moved close, holding tight to my arm as we came up the walk between the tall, dead hollyhock stalks, our quarrel forgotten.

It was a day for people to look older. Exactly my age, Alene Johnson looked more like Ma. She met us at the door, her eyes dull and red from crying. She brightened some when she saw me.

"Oh, Bud, thank you for coming."

She drew me inside, Ann following. Mrs. Winslow, the preacher's wife, was sitting on the sofa holding little Beth. Beth saw me and waved her arms, laughing, and that made Alene cry again.

"Do you think—will she remember him?" she asked me.

It took a second for me to understand, and another second to think what to say.

"Remember her daddy? Sure she will. You bet. We all will." About then I needed to wash my face again, but I set my jaw and managed not to make a fool of myself. I thought I'd made it through the hardest part.

But two days later at the cemetery, after Brother Winslow had preached Davy's funeral and the others had straggled away from the grave, Alene asked me the question she'd been saving.

"Bud, you have to tell me something about—about Davy."

I saw it again in my mind, the way it had been when I'd knelt beside Davy. The blood seemed more red and bright, like the winter sunlight was inside my mind.

"You don't want to hear about it, Alene."

She shook her head. "No," she said quickly. "Not that. Just—did he say anything? Did he mention—me?"

I looked past her, past the rows of tall tombstones and the white wooden crosses in the Mexican section. A rider I didn't know was sitting his horse just outside the back fence. His hat was slanted down against the afternoon sun, but he seemed to be staring toward a new grave apart from the rest.

"He did," I told Alene. "Just at the last, he whispered my name. I bent down, and he said, 'Tell Alene I love her.' And little Beth. He said that, too."

It wasn't much of a lie; Davy would have said it if he'd had time. Alene cried for a minute with me holding her, and then she stopped. She lifted her black veil, wiped her eyes, and took my arm to catch up with the others. By the time it came to me to wonder who had been so interested in Trey Bonner's grave, the rider and his chestnut horse were gone.

Chapter 3

After the funeral Judge Poe held an inquest. Pretty near everybody within a day's ride must have crowded into that big courtroom to hear me testify. As soon as it was done I lit out. I didn't have much idea where I was going, but I'd had enough of people for a while.

I stopped at the farm to put up some supplies. I'd been paying Will Stanton ten cents a day to tend the mules and milk the cow, and he was glad to keep it up a few more days. When I went to refill the grub box on my wagon, there in the boot was the last thing I'd wanted to see—my rifle. I thought about my promise to bury it, but in the end I left it where it was.

I went to a place where I'd hunted, a high meadow back in the hills where I wasn't likely to see anyone else. Into the third day I stayed up there. I'd wanted to get it set in my mind that I'd never see Davy again, and that I hadn't done anything wrong by shooting his killer. From what the sheriff said, Trey Bonner had needed killing, but that didn't make me feel a lot better about what I'd done.

Mornings, before first light, deer that I didn't want to shoot drifted hesitantly along the edge of the woods at the lower end of the clearing, their long ears poised and twitching in my direction. A big red-tailed hawk spent the first day watching me from an oak limb, then decided I was harmless and went to work hunting mice across the meadow. Nights, I stared into my campfire and saw the man I'd killed smoldering in the coals. I didn't sleep much, and my dreams weren't anything to talk about. Every little bit I'd wake up to the sound of that ax blade, or to Davy's scream.

Late the second night a blue norther came up. I toughed it out until daylight, huddled in my old mackinaw with a blanket wrapped around my shoulders, but a man can't do his best thinking with the wind cutting right through him. When the sky started getting light I gave it up and came home. That wasn't much better. The wind whined around the eaves of the old house, catching under shingles and sounding for all the world like somebody meddling around outside. After I'd finished my supper I lay awake for an hour or more, trying to sort out the noises. Later I dreamed of the deer in the meadow and of Ann, a better dream than any I'd had since the shooting.

Next morning the norther had blown itself out. I remembered the night sounds long enough to scout around the yard. If anybody had been there, he hadn't left tracks, and anybody who'd prowl around a farmhouse at night in a hard freeze would suffer more than it would be worth to him anyway. I was doing my morning chores in the barn when I heard horses coming.

Anytime before I would've walked out to see who my company was. That morning my first thought was for my rifle. I'd left it in the house, so I opened the barn door a crack and peered out. Sheriff Stanton and Will were reining up beside my front porch. The sheriff glanced toward the barn, then turned his back to it as he stepped down from his horse. Feeling silly, I went out to say hello.

"Hi, Bud," Will sang out the moment he saw me. With the two of them side by side, I saw he was a younger tintype of his pa, the way Ann took after her ma in looks. "Did you get him?"

"Will." From when I was fourteen myself, I recognized the warning in Sheriff Stanton's slow voice. "I told you to forget that nonsense."

"Find who?" I asked.

Will glanced at his father. "Nobody. We didn't know if you'd got home yet. I just came to feed the stock."

"Why'n't you go do that, son? I'll just wait and have a word with Bud."

I started to say the chores were about finished but changed my mind. Amos Stanton hadn't ridden five miles on a cold morning for nothing. He had something to say. My first thought was that it was about Ann—maybe that the sheriff didn't want a man-killer courting his daughter. I waited until Will had run off toward the barn, then inclined my head toward the house.

"Coffee's on, Sheriff. Care to come in?"

"That'd be mighty welcome, Bud. Mornings seem colder the past few years. Everything all right out here?"

The first part was just visiting, but the question came with a sharp look. I nodded as I led the way inside.

"Sure. Why do you ask?"

"Well, I didn't remember you were in the habit of peeping out of your own barn."

I motioned the sheriff to a seat at the kitchen table, then went to set the coffeepot back on the stove. I took a little longer than I needed to, just so he wouldn't see the red rising into my face.

"Shoot," I said. "I got spooked is all—thought somebody was prowling around last night."

The sheriff frowned but didn't say anything. I thought it was time to change the subject.

"What was it Will was saying? Who was I supposed to find?"

Amos Stanton tugged at his mustache. "It was nothing. Just town talk, always the same riffraff spreading gossip." He took the cup I offered him. "You shouldn't worry about it."

"*What* shouldn't I worry about?"

He hesitated, then sighed. "Well, when you left town the word went around you were out hunting for Trey Bonner's partner, the one that got away."

"That would be pretty silly, seeing as I don't even know what he looked like."

"Like I said, town talk." He was silent for a little while, warming his hands on the cup. "Trey Bonner, now, no doubt about him. Likely his price will come to three, four hundred dollars."

"Price?"

"Reward. You've got it coming; I've already filed the papers, so in a month or two—"

I turned away, pretending to refill my cup. It didn't need refilling. Fact is, I felt sick.

"I don't want it."

"Ann tells me you've thought of raising draft animals here. That money could start a nice little breeding herd."

The sickness passed, and I could feel red mounting to my face again, hot and angry. "Blood money." I slammed my cup down and turned back to the sheriff. "I'm not some bounty killer."

He might not have heard. "Or a man could take a trip, or pay off a farm." He studied me, expressionless. "Get married, even, like Davy did."

"Listen, I don't want to get married bad enough to—"

By the time I heard how that sounded, I could see little smile marks at the corners of his eyes. My head hadn't been any too clear, but all at once I thought I heard what he was trying to tell me.

"That's good," I said, understanding. "I'm glad you sent for the money. It was Davy that earned it, and Alene's going to need it with a kid to look after."

The sheriff dipped his head. "That's a right generous idea, Bud," he said in that slow way of his. "Glad you thought of it. By the way, there's a deputy's job—"

"Hey!" That was Will, still outside. The barn door slammed, and a second later he landed on the front porch. "Hey, Bud, you sent me on a snipe hunt. You'd already fed the animals." He came inside, scowling at his pa. "I get it. You wanted to tell Bud yourself."

Amos Stanton gave his son another of those frowns, but it didn't do any good.

"That's what he did, ain't it, Bud? He didn't want me to tell you, did he? About the town meeting next Sunday."

"Town meeting?" I looked at Will, then back at the sheriff. "What about?"

I never did get a straight answer from Will and the sheriff. The rest of the town, when I drove in Saturday for supplies, wasn't much better. In the mercantile, Todd Milner grinned at me the whole time he was filling my order. Homer Moore, down at the Owl

Barber Shop, talked a blue streak while he trimmed my hair but never mentioned the meeting. When I asked him about it straight out, he adjusted his rimless spectacles and clicked his scissors busily.

"Oh, you know how Judge Poe is when it gets to be speech-making time. I don't suppose anybody in town knows *exactly* what he's got to say."

"Well, I don't suppose anybody will notice if I don't show up, then."

Homer went to fiddling among his big square-faced bottles of bay rum and brilliantine and Magic Hair Elixir. "Oh, I expect they'd notice," he said, chuckling a little. "You don't want to miss it, Bud, believe me."

Whatever he said, I wasn't interested in the meeting. It didn't take a railroad detective to see I was involved, and I was pretty well determined to stay clear of it. When I said so to Pa, though, he frowned and looked at the ground.

"Bud, I'd take it kindly if you'd sit through it with us." He rested his hand on the edge of the wagon seat and looked up at me. From his tone, I knew he didn't much like what he was saying. "Judge Poe said he meant to talk about something of special concern to me."

Those were the judge's words, I could tell. I was still half-minded to say no, but Pa always hated to ask anybody for a favor, and he didn't ask for many.

"Surely." I pressed my lips together, then shrugged. All right, that was done. "Well, I'll see you in the morning, then."

"That's fine. Good night, son."

Sunday I got my morning chores done early, then brushed myself down and put on my suit for church. By the time I got there everybody else was already inside. Ma and Pa had waited for me, so we trooped in and took seats away down front. Ann was in the middle of the choir, where I could keep my eyes on her when Brother Winslow swung into his sermon, all about violence and the power of love. I listened as best I could, but Annette was right there, pretty as a bride in her new bonnet. While the preacher talked about loving and forgiving I started to think about being fruitful and multiplying. Ann caught my eye once, then looked down to blush, as if the same idea might have occurred to her. It was a mighty scriptural time, and it wasn't until people started standing up that I realized Brother Winslow had called for the closing hymn.

Then old Judge Poe ambled up to the pulpit, and we went right into the meeting. The church and Finster's Barbary Palace were the only places in town big enough to hold a meeting, and even the Palace might not have held everybody that was coming in now. Almost the whole county seemed to be there, some from as far away as Rising Star. What surprised me most was when Luke MacNally and Johnnie slipped into a back pew. Johnnie was wearing her blue dress again. Looking at her, I remembered that not all my dreams lately had been about Annette.

"Folks!" Judge Poe looked around like he was searching for a gavel, then gave it up and raised his voice. "Folks, let's come to order, now."

The judge must have been near seventy, but his courtroom voice was strong as ever. He looked like an old eagle perched in the pulpit with his thin, bony face and his sharp eyes gazing out at us. Folks started to quiet down and turn toward him.

"I haven't come to make a speech today," he began. Somebody behind me snickered, but the judge ignored it. "As most of you know, we've gathered here to honor one of our finest young citizens for his heroic attempt to save the life of our own Deputy Davy Johnson. Without thought of his own safety, this courageous young man . . ."

I quit listening. It hadn't been a bit like the judge was telling it. I hadn't risked much of anything; after all, I'd had the rifle against Bonner's handgun, and I'd taken him by surprise. And I sure hadn't felt heroic or courageous at the time. Mostly I'd been sick and scared.

The folks around me couldn't see what had really happened, though. They saw it the way Judge Poe was spinning it out. They were craning their necks to get a look at me now, all grinning like I was a real hero.

I leaned toward Pa. "Why'd you let them do this to me?" I whispered.

He closed his hand gently on my knee, the way he'd used to do when I was ten and needed quieting.

"Bud, these people have spent time and money to show what they think of you. It wouldn't be right to take that away."

"What money?"

Sitting on the other side, Ma nudged me. "You, Bud," she whispered. "Hush, now."

I looked her way, and that was when I saw Alene Johnson, dressed all in black. Her eyes shone with tears while the judge talked about Davy, a fine lawman cut down in the flower of his promising life. Her pride was for Davy, but I was tied up in it too. Though I still wasn't happy, I knew Pa was right. Whatever was coming, I had to manage as best I could. Afterward, I'd be sure Alene got the reward, then wash my hands of the whole business.

". . . all know who I'm talking about." Like an eight-day clock, Judge Poe was starting to run down.

"Bud Tilden, come on up here where everybody can see you!"

He stretched out a thin, liver-spotted hand toward me, and everybody took that for a sign to clap and cheer. Then I was in the aisle and walking toward the chancel for the first time since I'd joined the church. The whole way I wondered what I was going to say.

The judge wasn't finished. With me up there beside him he read off a proclamation full of words like duty and law and valor. It ended up: ". . . in whose memory and honor we make this presentation." I figured it meant the reward.

Judge Poe reached into the shelf below the pulpit and pulled out a flat wooden box, oblong and shiny as a little coffin. He put it in my hands. It was dovetailed together so the joints hardly showed, and the wood was polished bright as a new boot.

"The whole community—all these people here—join together to offer you this token of their gratitude, Bud. Open it up and let everybody see."

I fumbled with the brass catches, then finally swung back the lid. Inside, cradled in a bed of dark blue velvet, was a brand new Colt Peacemaker revolver. The grips were ivory, carved with a Lone Star, and the nickeled barrel was engraved with my name and the date and something about grateful appreciation. Six shiny .44-40 cartridges lay in a little nest in the corner of the box. Except for Annette Stanton, it was about the prettiest thing I'd ever seen. I hated it.

"Uses the same shells as your carbine, Bud," Seth Crabtree yelled.

The people were all clapping again, and then some jackass hollered for a speech. It sounded like Will Stanton, and I promised myself I'd give him a good hiding for it. I laid the box on top of the pulpit. I wanted to tell them my family didn't hold with handguns, and that offering me a gun for killing a man was worse than offering money. But I couldn't say any of that.

"Thank—thank you all." I gulped. Everybody was watching. Ma was crying, and so were most of the other women. "Davy, though, he was really the brave one. He was doing his job the best he could. All I did was what any of you would've done. I just happened to be the one who was there, that's all."

"Modest, too." Judge Poe was beside me, wringing my hand in a powerful, bony grip. "I just want to say there's a deputy's job open for you whenever you want it. The sheriff and all the rest of us would be proud to see you take Davy's place. How about it, folks?"

After that, people crowded around the pulpit like bees swarming. I had to shake hands with every living soul there before I could get away. The last two were Johnnie MacNally and Luke. He was the youngest of the MacNally boys, just my age.

Johnnie's hand was firm and callused from working, but anybody could have told it was a girl's hand. She looked at me seriously, like she wanted to ask a question but wouldn't.

"Congratulations, Bud," she said. "I hope—"

She didn't say what she hoped. Before I had time to wonder abbout it, Luke growled, "I don't see as you done anything so special."

My face was about to bust from smiling, so it was a pleasure to stop. "Luke," I told him, "this one time, you and I see things just alike." Then I got past him, up the aisle and out the door, away from all those others who wanted to make me out a hero.

I ducked around the corner of the church and ran for Mr. Hart's old stable. Inside it, the world was still and warm, with the smells of hay and dust and leather coming from the rotting harness hanging on the walls. I climbed up into the loft and made myself a place in the hay. After a little while I heard people moving around outside, their talk dying away as the crowd broke up and went home. Then one of the big front doors creaked open enough to let in a streak of light.

"Bud?"

The door swung closed again, but I could hear her breathing inside. It was Annette. Nobody else would have known where to look for me. She knew because we had sneaked off there sometimes when we were kids to play and talk and whatnot. That loft was where I'd gotten my first kiss from her.

"Bud, are you here? Please answer me."

"In the loft."

"Can I come up?"

"Sure."

She came up the ladder, paying no mind to her modesty or her Sunday dress. Ducking under the rafters, she folded herself lightly down beside me and pulled loose the ribbon under her chin to take off her bonnet. Little bars of afternoon sun came through the cracks in the roof to shine on her golden hair.

She put out her hand to cover mine. "You didn't like it, did you?"

"The gun?"

"All the attention. I could tell."

She ducked her head and lifted my hand to her lips. "Does it still bother you? The shooting?" she asked.

I didn't say anything. I guess I didn't have to.

"What the judge and the others said, didn't that help? They want you to be a lawman, like Papa."

"They weren't there, Ann. They don't know how it was."

"Can I help?"

"You don't know either."

That must have hurt her, though I hadn't meant to. "I know I'm proud of you," she said defiantly.

I rolled over so I could see her face. She looked solemn, but her eyes hoped I'd smile so she could, too. All of a sudden, what I needed most in the world was to hold her real close and not have to think any more. I reached up, pulled her down on top of me. She gave a little squeal, more in surprise than protest, and then we were lying quiet in the hay with my arms tight around her. I kissed her and felt her mouth fit itself against mine.

"Oh, Bud," she whispered.

I knew we'd better stop, but what I knew didn't seem to help much. Times past, we'd played at loving in the loft, just kids being daring. We weren't kids now, and there was nothing playful about the way I felt. I drew her head down and kissed her again, sliding one hand to press the bodice of her dress. Through the cloth, her breast was soft and alive.

"Bud," she breathed again, sounding more eager and more desperate than before. I saw fear in her eyes, but there was excitement, too, and pride. Her look said I was somebody new, somebody she'd never seen before—a hero.

That hit me like a bucket of creek water on a frosty morning. I moved away from her and sat up, tightening my arms around my knees.

"I'm not any hero," I said.

Her face tightened like I'd slapped her. "That wasn't why!" she said. She started brushing hay off her dress, not looking at me. "It was—Bud, I—I care for you."

I couldn't say anything. After a minute she found her bonnet and tied it on crooked. Then she fished around in the hay and came up with that polished wooden box.

"You left this."

When I didn't reach out for it she set it on the hay beside me. She went halfway down the ladder, then came back to where her head showed over the top.

"Well, I don't care. I'm going to be proud of you anyway!"

"Ann? I'm sorry."

"Me, too."

Before I could decide what she meant she slid down the ladder like a kid. At the door she turned to look up. "I love you, Bud," she said, just loud enough for me to hear. Probably I would've answered her, but she didn't wait. The hinges groaned, and she was gone.

I picked up the box. It didn't really look so much like a coffin. Not wanting to, I snapped the lid open again. The Colt's nickel plating caught the sunlight like a silver snake, and its ivory grips settled into my hand as if I'd been born holding them. Thumbing back the smooth-working hammer was natural as breathing—but I didn't breathe. If Pa had taught me anything, it was to stay clear of handguns.

Of course, he'd taught me the same thing about whiskey.

Chapter 4

FOR A WEEK OR SO I would've kept to myself, if folks had let me. I set out to clear the brush from the hillside pasture, but there wasn't a day when somebody didn't come to visit. It didn't seem unusual at first. Dr. Wisenhunt stopped in on his way back to town from tending old Mrs. Doolin. Then Sheriff Stanton turned up, just out looking after the county. Even Brother Winslow's visit could be explained.

"You know, Bud, I get around to see most of the flock every few months. Good coffee; you'll rival your mother one of these days. Since I happened to be out this way, I thought I'd pay you a call."

"Glad you did. And thank Mrs. Winslow for sending the cake. Sure you won't join me for a slice?"

"Oh, no, thank you." He set his cup and saucer on his knee and smiled carefully. "I suppose you were pleased with the town meeting."

"I suppose."

"I didn't vote for the gun."

"No?" I looked at him, surprised by how sudden

he'd brought it up. Talking with Brother Winslow was generally a roundabout business.

"No. Neither did your father."

"It's like paying me for killing."

His hands moved in distress. "That's not how they saw it, Bud." He hesitated a second. "I've changed my mind. If you won't tell Mrs. Winslow, just this once, I believe I will have a taste of that cake."

"I won't let on." I cut a slab of the chocolate cake, dark and rich as bottomland, and put it on a saucer for him. "About the Colt—just how *did* they mean it?"

"They wanted to show their approval."

"Of killing?"

"Of you." He took out his handkerchief and wiped chocolate from his beard. "These are good people, Bud, most of them. It isn't their fault if they're trying to make you into something you're not. Nor your fault either, if you don't want to change."

"What are they trying to make me into?"

"A lawman, I'd say. That's what the judge suggested, and I'm sure Sheriff Stanton agrees."

I laughed. "It's not for me, Preacher," I said. "I doubt I could change anyway. I've never meant to be anything except a farmer."

"I understand."

"What did you vote for—a Bible?"

"A new seven-inch breaking plow."

That caught me flat-footed, and I stared at him. "You knew I needed a plow?" I asked.

"Wonderful coffee, Bud, but such small cups. Thank you." He looked up as I brought the coffeepot back. His smile was different this time, like he was laughing at the both of us. "I told you I understood. I never intended to be anything except a farmer, either."

* * *

On Saturday I gave it up and drove into town for supplies. With Christmas coming on, I needed something I could give for presents without spending money I didn't have. My old carbine was across my knees, not for protection but to remind me to take it to Avery Thomas, our gunsmith. I'd finally noticed its extractor was broken, probably from the knocking around it had taken that night at the Wells. A spent shell was still lodged in the chamber.

Pulling up in front of Todd Milner's mercantile, I started to leave the rifle on the wagon seat. I'd always been taught it wasn't smart to leave guns lying around, though, broken or not, so I took it with me up the porch steps and through the wide double door of the mercantile.

Just in the doorway a man coming out ran spang into me. It staggered me a little, but not as much as him, because he was carrying a big box of groceries. He looked to be about my age, but shorter and with thick, black hair. He wasn't anybody I'd ever seen there before, but he was wearing a white storekeeper's apron.

"Sorry," I said. He'd fallen back a step or two, bent over and scrabbling to keep from dropping the box. I had the rifle in my right hand, so I reached out with my left. "Let me help you with that."

"I've got it," he snapped. He straightened, glaring at me. "You ought—"

He stopped dead, looking first at me, then at the Winchester. His face went pale, and he jerked back like he was burned. The grocery box crashed on the wood floor. A cloud of flour puffed up from it like smoke, but he didn't seem to notice. He was still staring at me.

"Well, I hope you don't expect me to pay for that

bag." The widow Mabry was right behind him. She flapped a hand to clear away the flour. "Land's sake, young man, he's not here to rob the store. This here is Bud Tilden. You must know about him."

"I know about him."

"Here, what's the matter?" Todd Milner came bustling from somewhere in the back. "What happened, Stone?"

"I dropped—" the one called Stone began, but Widow Mabry cut him off.

"He saw Bud's gun and it scared him, that's all," she said. From his face, he didn't like that any, but she didn't notice. "I hope you don't expect me to pay for that flour."

"No, ma'am. Stone, fix up Miz Mabry's order again. And that bag of flour comes out of your pay."

"It was my fault, Todd," I said. "Put the flour on my bill."

"No." The new clerk straightened. He had color back in his face now. "I have the money. I'll not be beholden to you for anything."

He scooped up the box and turned away without a glance back at any of us. Widow Mabry clucked her tongue.

"Well, I never!"

"We'll get your order right over, ma'am," Todd said, walking her toward the door. "Don't you fret, now."

When she was gone he came back to look over my list. "Coffee, sugar, hmmm. All this flavoring and candied fruit, you must be planning big doings for Christmas."

"Well, if I am, I'd rather the whole town didn't know about it." I sounded sharper than I'd meant. I nodded toward the back. "Who's your new clerk?"

"Name's Braden, Stone Braden. New in town.

Good worker, seems honest." He looked up from the list and grinned. "Little bit sullen, ain't he?"

"Little bit," I agreed. "Oh, I need a box of .44-40s."

He took a pencil from behind his ear and made a note. "For that new pistol, eh? Mighty nice."

"For the carbine."

"Oh, yeah. Sure." He chuckled. "Forgot how modest all you Tildens are."

While Todd put my order together I went across to Finster's Barbary Palace. I'd never been inside it—nor any other saloon, for that matter—and it wasn't my idea of a palace. The inside looked and smelled worse than the outside. A few men were sitting at the tables, but I didn't pay them much mind; nobody but trash was likely to be drinking at that time of morning. Instead, I walked up to the long bar and laid my Winchester on top of it, careful not to scratch the wood.

Finster—if he had a first name, nobody had ever found it out—turned from studying himself in the mirror. He was a thin, dried-up man with a glass eye. Seeing him had always made me feel half of him was looking off into the distance while the other half watched things like a cat at a mouse hole.

"Need something, friend?"

"A quart of rum."

He frowned. "That'd be two dollars, was I to sell it." He folded his arms. "But I ain't. You not being used to it, you'd make an ass of yourself in public. Then the church ladies would give the sheriff hell until he closed me down."

I doubted the ladies would make such a fuss, since Finster had been the biggest contributor to build a parsonage. I fished for two silver dollars and slid them to him.

"It's all right. I don't aim to drink it."

"What ya gonna do, boy, use it for hair tonic?"

The voice was slurred but familiar. I turned around to see who it had come out of. Luke MacNally was sitting at one of the tables. The two men with him were strangers to me, but it didn't take an Indian scout to figure them as trouble. Luke had a half-empty glass in his hand.

"Let him be, Luke," Finster said quickly. He reached without looking and took down a bottle from the shelves beside the mirror. "Here, Bud, take this and get along."

"Bud?"

Luke pushed himself up from the table, staggering a little. A gunbelt rode at his waist. The other two moved fast to spread out a couple of steps to either side. Both of them had pistols showing under their coats. That was bad. Not many men in Comanche carried handguns day to day, and those that did usually had a reason.

"Bud who?"

"Just be still, Luke," Finster said, like he was quieting a baby. "You don't want trouble—not in here. Just sit down, now, until you can see better."

"Is that you, Bud?"

"It's me, Luke. We've got no quarrel."

"It's Bud Tilden, Luke," Finster said. "You and your friends just sit back down, now."

"Why, hell, Bud." Luke laughed, swaying so he had to hold to the back of his chair. "It's got plumb dark in here. I didn't know that was you."

In the back, a man cackled laughter—old Seth Crabtree, I thought. "I'll just bet you didn't," he crowed.

One of the men with Luke muttered something, and

then the two of them sifted through the others and out the back door. Luke was still blinking in my direction.

"Don't you think I'm afraid of you, Bud."

"I don't think that."

"See, Luke?" Finster moved away from me along the bar. "He don't think that."

Crabtree cackled again. "He don't think it's cold out, neither," he mocked. "Not much he don't!"

Finster's voice got sharp. "Shut up, Crabtree. Leave it alone."

I was starting to think it wasn't my day. First there had been Stone Braden, and now Luke. I picked up the bottle in one hand and took my carbine in the other.

"That your rifle?" Luke asked. "I ain't afraid. My partners might be, but I'm not."

"He knows you're not," Finster said. "We all know."

I started for the door. Luke yelled once more, but I didn't turn around. Behind me in the saloon men were laughing. I headed toward the gunsmith's, just wanting to walk and breathe deep. If she hadn't dodged me, I'd have run right over Johnnie MacNally.

In her jeans and work coat she looked like the Johnnie I knew. She stepped in front of me when I stopped, her hands on her hips and her mouth a tight line. She was looking at the bottle in my hand.

"It's not to drink," I said.

From her expression I knew I'd gotten crossways with another MacNally. She jerked her head toward Finster's door.

"Is Luke in there?"

It didn't seem fair to turn her loose on Luke right then. "I'm not sure," I said, telling my conscience he might have followed his friends out the back way.

"Hmmph! No sense asking one drunk about another."

Johnnie's tone made it clear what she thought about drinking in general and me in particular. She whirled away and strode toward Finster's like she meant to go inside. When it came to me that was just what she did mean, I went after her.

"Johnnie! Wait a minute, you can't—"

About that time, something like a grizzly bear took me by the collar and swung me out of the way. I'd been carrying the rum under the same arm that held my rifle. Now the bottle slipped out and smashed on the steps of the Barbary Palace.

"Johnnie," the bear said, "don't you set one foot inside that place."

I turned around, mad. "Now, look here," I began. "That bottle cost me—"

Two dollars, I'd meant to say, but when I saw the bear was Johnnie's older brother Matthew I swallowed the rest of it. Matthew was big and heavyset like his pa had been. His face was pretty much covered with a dark brown beard that made him seem ten years older than me instead of five. Looking at the parts of him that showed, I saw he wasn't in much of a mood for conversation.

At the sound of Matthew's voice Johnnie had stopped dead. "I'm going after Luke," she said, but she wasn't nearly as sassy with him as she'd been with me.

Matthew didn't answer her. Instead, he turned to me. His size and his steady blue eyes made him look hard and dangerous, which he was. His thick-lipped mouth, usually a little bit open, made him look stupid, which he wasn't. He was one of those few men who always went around armed, though I'd never found a good time to ask him why.

"Luke in there?"

"He was a while ago."

"Two men with him?"

"They went out the back."

To Johnnie he said, "I'll handle it." Then he trod over the broken pieces of my bottle and went into the Palace. Things got mighty quiet inside.

Finster's doorway didn't seem to be a good place to stay. "I'm going to see Avery Thomas," I told Johnnie. "I'd be honored if you'd walk along with me." When she hesitated I added, "I don't think Matthew wants us here."

She frowned but fell in beside me. "I'm glad your bottle got broken," she said, looking at me from the corners of her eyes.

"I'll get another one," I said. "And I wanted to ask your help with it." She stopped in her tracks. "No, for Christmas presents."

"Bud! That's blasphemous!"

I opened my mouth, then closed it again. She'd taken root right on the spot, her arms folded and her eyes flashing anger.

"Listen," I said. "What we're going to do is to start over. What I meant to say at first was, 'Miss MacNally, you looked mighty pretty in that blue dress.' "

Anybody who's seen metal melt would understand the change in her face. Her smile made me think of sunlight coming through after a rainstorm. For just that minute she looked like the girl I'd surprised in Ma's doorway the day after Davy was shot. Then her smile clouded over again.

"I suppose that means I'm ugly in my regular clothes."

Talking to her was sort of like breaking mules to harness, except I've never run across a mule that contrary. "You always look pretty," I said. "I shoul-d've said the blue dress was very becoming."

"Thank you." She narrowed her eyes suspiciously. "Why are you shining up to me? Did you and Ann have a fight?"

"No. And I'm not. But I did start out to ask you a favor."

Her expression was wary. "What . . ." she began. Then she looked past me, and I felt the boards of the sidewalk tremble under my feet. When I turned around Matthew was standing there, Luke draped across his shoulder like a shawl.

"Johnnie." His voice was nice enough, but he was watching me instead of her. "Bring the wagon, please."

"Did he pass out again?" she asked.

"Sort of. He wasn't quite ready to leave. Go on, now."

Johnnie went, leaving me to entertain Matthew. Nothing of Luke was showing except his boots and his backside, but I could tell he wouldn't be much company for a while. I don't know what had happened to his pistol.

"You were speaking awful serious to Johnnie," Matthew observed. "You ought to be careful about that—most especially since I've heard you mean to marry Annette Stanton. Mark and Luke and me, we'd hate to think somebody was dealing lightly with Johnnie's affections."

The way he said that, all careful and polite, it should've been funny. I didn't have any urge at all to laugh. It was a wonder how he could be talking along with Luke balanced on his shoulder like a sack of feathers.

"I was asking her help," I said. "I'm baking some fruitcakes for Christmas, and I'm not very good at it."

He didn't say anything, so I explained how I didn't have much ready money this time of year, but I wanted to give something to Ma and Pa and some others, and that I'd bought supplies and the rum because making fruitcakes had seemed like a good idea. It didn't sound so good while I was telling him about it, but I sure kept his attention.

"I don't do enough baking to mention," he said slowly when I'd finished. "But I'm morally certain you don't put rum in fruitcakes. I think you're trying to be clever."

That was about enough, even if it was Matthew. He'd come mighty near to calling me a liar. "Think whatever you want to," I said. "You're the third MacNally today looking to sharpen his claws on me, and I don't think I'm going to get so's I like it."

He eyed me calmly while Johnnie pulled the wagon up right beside us. Then he went over and dumped Luke on top of a dozen bags of grain. I noticed he never quite turned his back on me while he was doing it.

"Johnnie, take him home," he said. "I've got a bit more business here. Likely Luke will wake up before I get there. If he doesn't, just leave him be."

"I'm not ready to go home," Johnnie said. "I'm not through shopping."

"John Catherine."

Johnnie looked at me, daring me to laugh. Then she made a face at Matthew.

"Matthew, when are you going to quit trying to be our daddy?"

"When you're a woman grown. Now get along home!"

Johnnie didn't like that, and neither did I. She snapped the reins over the horses' rumps, and the wagon started off with a jolt. Matthew had to jump to get his feet clear of the iron tires. I liked that.

Soon as Johnnie was gone I found out about the rest of Matthew's business. "I'm told you were leaning on Luke pretty hard," he said.

I stared at him, so surprised that I forgot all about being mad. Finally I said, "Whoever told you that is mistaken."

"It's said you tried to stir him up, made him look foolish in front of the saloon crowd."

I thought of Crabtree, and I remembered Sheriff Stanton's words. "Town talk," I said. "Saloon talk."

"Maybe. Bear in mind, any trouble with Luke is trouble with Mark and me. MacNallys stick with their kin."

"MacNallys ought to keep their kin out of saloons, then," I said. His face darkened, but I kept going. "Matthew, in all the years you've known me, do you remember me *ever* provoking a fight with you or your brothers?"

"No," he admitted. Then his voice went hard. "That was before you got yourself a name as a man-killer."

"I'm not proud of it. And I don't mean to start trouble with anybody."

"That why you're carrying your carbine?"

I looked down at the Winchester. In all the commotion I'd about forgotten I was holding it. "It won't shoot," I said.

"Then you took an awful chance with Luke."

I tossed him the rifle. He caught it with his left hand and moved his right toward his holster. "That's fine," he said. "Now take that pretty silver Colt out of whatever pocket it's in, and let's start even."

"I don't carry a handgun." I let my voice show what I thought about folks who did. "I'm taking the carbine to Avery Thomas. If you'll open the action, you can see for yourself."

He studied me a second longer, then yanked down the carbine's lever. Another second, and he closed it and threw the rifle back to me. I caught it with both hands.

"Extractor's broke," Matthew said. It was the first time he'd sounded like he knew me. "You took an awful chance," he repeated thoughtfully.

"I didn't know Luke was in there, let alone drunk," I said. "Listen, you or Mark whipped me a few times when we were kids; probably you could do it now if you wanted to. I whipped Luke a few times; probably I could do it now if I had to. I'd rather have neighbors than enemies. That's up to you."

He almost grinned. "You always were sort of feisty, Bud," he said. "I don't suppose you've changed so much." Then his face got serious. "You've earned a name as a shooter now. You're a good man to try and dodge it—I'll give you that—but you can't. It'll follow you all your days." He went quiet again, but he wasn't finished. "Best you go get that carbine fixed. There'll be somebody along to make you use it."

I shook my head. "Not likely. I don't mean to spend the rest of my life carrying a gun and looking over my shoulder."

I figured that would make him mad. Instead, he grinned and looked away.

"It won't matter so much whether you carry it or not," he said, his voice almost gentle. "Only difference'll be how long you mean by 'the rest of your life.' "

Chapter 5

JOHNNIE MACNALLY SHOWED UP on my front porch just after breakfast Monday morning. Under a long wool coat she was wearing her work clothes. "I'm ready," she said.

The first thing I'd noticed was that she didn't need the blue dress to make her pretty. I didn't tell her so because brother Matthew was right there beside her.

"Johnnie has agreed to go along with this fruitcake nonsense," he greeted me. "I expect you'll remember what I told you on Saturday."

Meaning, I knew, that I was not to trifle with Johnnie's affections. That seemed almost funny. Johnnie had never struck me as a lady it would be safe to trifle with, even if she didn't have three older brothers. But I made it plain I understood Matthew. He took time to look over the kitchen, poking around the sacks of flour and sugar like a bear going through a grub box.

"I'll be around should you need me," he said finally. Then he mounted his dun gelding—supposed to be the fastest horse in the county—and rode away.

Johnnie had already taken off her hat and coat. Unfolding a well-worn piece of paper, she began to make her own check of the supplies like a bear cub.

"I'll need spices and some other things," she said. "I'll make a list."

"*We'll* need spices," I told her. "I asked you to help, was all."

She smiled. "Then maybe *we* should start with clean bowls and pans."

I didn't say anything. Living alone and with all the visitors I'd had, I'd gotten behind on dishwashing. Dishes can wait, but cows and mules and the like can't. I hauled in water for the dishpan while Johnnie built up a fire in the stove.

"I think we'll need some more stove wood, too," she said.

"Matthew said we should call him if we need help," I reminded her.

Johnnie laughed low and clear, like river water tumbling over pebbles. "Poor Matthew! He's got Luke working cattle back home. Between watching him and mothering me, he'll have that horse worn out."

"I wouldn't think you need much mothering," I said.

She brought the simmering water and poured it in the dishpan, standing so near me I could smell the freshness of her hair.

"Matthew thinks so." She looked slantwise at me. "He says it isn't proper for me to be alone with a man this way. There's no telling what might happen."

"Well, he's right."

"Is he?" Her smile was a question, as full of mischief as a little girl's, but tensed like a cat ready to run for cover. I felt my face get red.

"He's right to worry about you, I mean. Around any man."

"I can take care of myself." She tossed her head and moved away. "Besides, I don't see any other man around here. You're the one he's wondering about."

"Never mind him," I said. "What about you? You aren't afraid of me, are you?"

She shook her head. "I wondered why you asked me, was all. I'd have thought you'd ask Annette." She watched me, little girl and cat all mixed together. "This is going to be her kitchen some day, isn't it?"

I had the feeling I'd taken a wrong fork, but there was no place wide enough to turn around. I rolled up my sleeves and went to work in the soapy dishwater.

"She's one of the ones I wanted to surprise. With the cakes."

To my surprise, Johnnie laughed. "I expect you will," she said. I looked at her, but the cat had gone away and her face was all little-girl innocence.

When we had the kitchen ready for her to begin I headed out to pick up the things on her list. Fact is, I was glad for an excuse to go to town. I'd been thinking over what Judge Poe had said about the deputy's job, and I thought I might stop in for a word with the sheriff. Matthew was sitting his horse on the ridge above the barn, so I knew Johnnie would be safe enough while I was gone.

"Hurry, now," Johnnie called from the porch as I was leaving. "I can't finish until you get back."

"Don't worry," I told her. "I won't be long."

Which just goes to show how wrong a body can be sometimes.

Like always on a Monday morning, Milner's store was busy. Everybody knew the farmers and ranchers came in for supplies on Saturday, so the town ladies did their shopping on Monday. A goodly number of men had gathered just to visit while they ate crackers and pickles and cheese cut from the big yellow wheel Todd Milner always kept out on the counter. Todd was waiting on customers, but his new clerk, Stone Braden, was nowhere in sight. That suited me well enough. I took out my list and started gathering things on my own.

About the time I'd finished Seth Crabtree led another little group of people in. That surprised me, because Crabtree mostly spent his waking hours—and some of the sleeping ones, too—over at Finster's. It was a surprise when he came right up to me and offered his hand.

"Thought that was your wagon, Bud Tilden. Mighty glad to see you, yes, sir."

My nose told me he'd just come from the saloon. I shook his hand, figuring I could wash up later. The ones who'd come in with him stood back, watching without a word, and some of the other folks started to look at us curiously. Then a man I didn't know pushed out of Crabtree's crowd and planted himself in front of me.

"You're Bud Tilden?"

"That's right." I put down my goods on the counter and offered my hand. He didn't take it. "I don't believe I know you."

"Name's Mayfield. Orren Mayfield."

He hooked his thumbs in his belt and waited like he expected that to mean something to me. It didn't. He was lean and strung taut like a Comanche bow. He wore a dark blue shirt with white sleeve garters above the elbows. The butt of a pistol stuck out of the waistband of his jeans. His face sort of pinched in toward the middle, making him look like some kind of hawk. Up close he wasn't much older than me. His eyes were cold and gray and steady on my face.

"What can I do for you?" I asked. I noticed things had gotten quiet, except where Todd was still asking Mrs. Cryer what kind of lace she wanted.

"Bud," Mayfield said thoughtfully. "Bud's sort of a boy's name. I was expecting a man." He looked over at the spices and candied fruit I'd put down. "Still got a sweet tooth, have you?"

Now even Todd was quiet, turning to see what was going on. I'd been raised to be polite, but something told me there wasn't enough politeness in the world to make Mayfield happy. I didn't waste any.

"Come a long way to inquire about my teeth, have you?"

He surprised me with a tight smile. "That's right," he said. "All the way from Palestine."

Off to one side, Seth Crabtree cackled out that laugh of his. "Mr. Mayfield, he's come a long way, Bud." He poked another of the barflies with his skinny elbow. "He was mighty all-fired anxious to meet the man who killed Trey Bonner."

Mayfield turned his eyes on Crabtree. "I'll do my own talking," he said. When he looked back at me his smile was gone. "The Mayfields and the Bonners are sort of cousins back in East Texas. I came to see the dirty murdering coward who bushwhacked one of my kin. Are you the one?"

I didn't like the question. "I shot him," I said.

"You murdered him. Else you'd never have put five bullets into Trey without him getting off a shot."

Somebody had been talking a lot. "The second man fired at me," I said. "Maybe you know all about that."

"Maybe I do."

"Then maybe you know Bonner killed a deputy—

chopped him down with an ax. I was just trying to stop it."

"That ain't what I heard."

I glanced at Crabtree. Town talk. "Then you heard wrong," I said.

"I don't think so." Mayfield squared himself around and dropped a hand toward the handle of his pistol. "I think you're a yellow-bellied liar."

"Hold on." I spread my hands. "I'm not armed."

Probably Mayfield didn't much care whether I had a gun or not. Seth Crabtree, though, chimed in right away.

"Not armed? Don't you got that pretty pistol we gave you?"

Now, I would've bet my horse that the whole Crabtree family hadn't contributed nine cents toward that pistol, but it didn't matter much at the moment. The only thing I could do was step closer to Mayfield. Hemmed in by the counter and the crowd behind him, he couldn't back away.

"Don't touch that pistol," I told him.

He grinned. "Like hell," he said, and he clawed for the gun.

I grabbed his wrist with my left hand and drove a right straight into his face. He clubbed at me left-handed in return, but I had him off balance. I got him again with my right, under the chin this time. His hat came off, and we fell to the floor together.

If I'd ever thought I could fight, Mayfield changed my mind for me in a hurry. As soon as he saw I wasn't going to let him get at his Colt he started to punch. He caught me with a couple of good shots, better than I'd hit him, and I felt my lips split open when he rammed the top of his head into my face. Still, while he'd been spending time looking tough in saloons, I'd been putting up hay or following a plow. If he was the better fighter, I had thirty more pounds of muscle. Also, I was on top, and that counts for a lot. I managed to rough him up pretty good, and when I was able to push away from him I had the Colt.

I stood up, holding the pistol loosely. Mayfield came to his hands and knees and began to give me a good gutter cussing.

"Shut up," I told him.

The words sounded pretty thick because my lips were swelling, but he understood. I dabbed at my chin, covering the back of my hand with blood. The crowd around us had gotten bigger during the fight, but nobody had offered to step in. Some of the men had even formed a ring around us, like they'd been betting on a cockfight. I looked at them until they had trouble meeting my eyes, then turned back to Mayfield.

"Whatever you wanted to prove, I hope that proved it." My mouth was bleeding all over my shirt, and my ribs felt like I'd been stepped on by a mule or two. "No, don't get up."

He didn't really want to anyway. He was still on hands and knees, with his head hanging down. I'd pounded it against the floor a few times during our scuffle, which hadn't improved his disposition any.

"Damned sodbuster," he muttered. Blood drooled from his mouth and made a puddle on the floor. When he looked up at me his face had gone white and his eyes were like a snake's. "Give me back my gun."

I lifted the Colt. It fit my hand nearly as well as the silver pistol, and I wondered why. I didn't want it. I couldn't very well hand it back to Mayfield, though, because he was in a killing mood if there ever was one. I shook my head—a mistake, because it felt like somebody had driven a railroad spike right through it.

"I guess not. I'll leave the pistol with Sheriff Stanton. You can ask him for it when you want to leave town."

"That's telling him, Bud!" somebody said from the crowd. The others took it up like it was something special. I stopped and looked at them. I don't know what my face was like, but it was enough to make them go quiet and back away. When I was sure they knew how I felt I turned my back on the whole bunch and started across toward the door.

I guess that shows how green I was. After all their big talk, nobody helped. Nobody yelled, not even Todd. The talk started up again, then cut off the way that ax had cut off Davy's scream. In the silence I heard Mayfield scrabbling around. Then came a sharp click, and that was all the warning I had.

Just as I started to turn there was a noise like two boards slapped together. A mule kicked me in the back, spinning me the rest of the way around, and I gagged on the smell of black powder. I didn't know what had happened until I saw Mayfield. He was up on his knees, struggling with a little hideout derringer to let the other barrel loose at me.

Just like at the Wells, I didn't think. His Colt was in my hand. I thumbed back the hammer as I swung it up, barely noticing the people scrambling for safety. I fired once, knowing it was wide, then shot again. The recoil carried my hand up. I couldn't see Mayfield for the smoke, but the derringer went off like a little cannon, and splinters raked my cheek. I brought the Colt down to where I figured the shot had come from and let it buck in my hand again. I still couldn't see—it must have gotten dark, I thought—but I heard a sound like a fish flopping on the bank.

"Plumb dead between the eyes! Some shooting, boys!"

That was Crabtree, leaning over Mayfield before

he'd even quit twitching. A score of voices all started up at once, men talking and women crying or screaming. I couldn't understand any of it, but I remembered their silence before. From the second I'd turned my back on Mayfield not a one of them had spoken a word to warn me. I wanted to tell them what I thought about that, but I tasted blood when I tried to speak. I choked on it, and then a heavy, black curtain settled down over me, and I lost track of things.

The next I knew I was lying on my stomach, looking down at the bare, scrubbed wooden floor of Doc Wisenhunt's surgery. Somebody was poking at my back with the devil's pitchfork. I couldn't tell who it was. I tried to turn and see, but a strong pair of hands caught my shoulders and held me still.

"Young fool!" I recognized the doc's voice, coming from pretty far away. He was grumpy as usual. "Just keep thrashing around there and you'll put yourself in Bethel Cemetery yet. Hold still!"

"Easy, Bud."

That was Sheriff Stanton. I guessed the hands belonged to him. All the talk was accompanied by some kind of activity that hurt like fury clear through my chest. I tried not to move. After what seemed like a month I heard something clunk in a pan on the floor.

"There, that's the bullet. You might even live—better fortune than you deserve. Don't you know better than to turn your back on a man like that?"

I will next time, I tried to say, but my voice wasn't working. Then a pair of boots moved into sight on the worn boards. Their owner hunkered down beside me, and I was looking into the lined face of Sheriff Stanton.

"The doctor thinks you'll be all right, Bud," he said. He tried to smile, but it didn't hide his worry.

"So I heard," I whispered. That didn't hurt so much.

"Don't butter him up," Doc Wisenhunt snapped. "That bullet fractured two ribs and bruised a lung. He'll likely spit blood for a while, but there should be no permanent damage." He leaned down to glare at me. "No fault of yours, young man. Nor any fault of that fellow who shot you. He did his best."

He held the bullet in a pair of forceps where I could see it. It was all whanged out of shape in a way that made me feel sick.

"Large caliber and low velocity," the doctor said. "Hell of a thing to shoot at a human being."

"It came mighty near getting the job done," Sheriff Stanton said quietly. "If you hadn't been turning around . . ." He left that thought unfinished. "Just say the Lord was watching after you."

"What about him?" Even the whisper was getting to be too much. Nobody could ever tell me a bullet doesn't hurt. "Mayfield?"

Wisenhunt and the sheriff looked at each other, then back at me. "He's dead," Doc said. "We thought you knew."

Like remembering a dream, I could hear Crabtree. "Right dead between the eyes." I had known Mayfield was dead, but that made me remember something else.

"They just let it happen," I muttered.

Probably I was half out of my mind, but the sheriff seemed to know exactly what I meant. The last I heard as I faded off to sleep was his soft voice.

"That's the way of it, son." I couldn't see his eyes, but I knew the sadness that was in them. "That's the way of it. They always do."

Chapter 6

THEY TOOK ME to my folks' house in the back of a wagon that didn't miss a bump or a rut the whole way. My insides were hurting enough that I should have had plenty to think about, but I couldn't get the shooting out of my mind. It wasn't like the first time. I didn't feel so bad about killing Orren Mayfield; it was the other folks in the store I kept remembering.

"They just let it happen," I heard myself repeating over and over, just like I'd said to Sheriff Stanton. Each time, I seemed to hear his answer. "That's the way of it, son. They always do."

Then somebody was carrying me inside, and Ma was bustling around with a lamp, clucking over me and leading the way to the spare bedroom.

"Now, don't be concerned, Mrs. Tilden," I heard Doc Wisenhunt saying. "He's a strong young man. This looks bad, but really it's only a scratch."

I don't know how the doc was accustomed to treating people who had more than a scratch—call the undertaker straight off, maybe—but Orren Mayfield's bullet made me doubt things I'd heard all my life. Pa had always hinted we had some Indian blood in the family, and old-timers claimed that Indians didn't notice pain. If that was true, the next couple of days showed me I didn't have enough Indian blood to make a meal for a mosquito. I don't remember much, except that everything hurt. On the third morning I woke up feeling improved enough to be measured for a coffin, and Ma came in humming "Rock of Ages" and carrying a bowl of watery oatmeal.

"Good morning, Bud. My, you're looking fine today."

She didn't mean a word of it. I tried to smile, but it was too much trouble. "I'm all right," I whispered.

"Why, sure you are. Maybe you can eat a little. And later I'll bet you'll be ready for a visitor."

That made me remember again. *"That's the way of it, son."*

"No. I don't want to see anybody."

"Not even Annette?"

That was different. "Yes. No, wait. I don't look fit to see her."

"Well, she isn't here yet, but she's been coming by every morning with that new deputy. We'll get you spruced up some—"

"New deputy?" Even sick, I didn't like the sound of that. "What new deputy?"

"Here, let me help you sit up. Does that hurt?"

"Yes. What new deputy?"

Ma finally seemed to hear me. "Oh, the sheriff hired that boy that was working at Milner's store," she said. "Brady, is it?"

"Braden. And he's not a boy. What's the sheriff doing, hiring some drifter like that?"

Ma looked at me in surprise. "Well, he seems like a

nice young man," she said. "A little quiet, that's all. Now finish your breakfast, and we'll get you ready to see Annette."

I stirred the oatmeal without eating much of it. Maybe I hadn't been too keen on the deputy's job when it was first offered, but I'd been thinking it over. I sure hadn't figured Amos Stanton would jerk the offer out from under me the minute I got hurt. Most of all, I couldn't see why he'd given Davy's badge to Stone Braden—a sullen newcomer who turned pale and dropped things at the sight of a rifle.

Probably I would've worked myself into a real state but for the promise of Annette's visit. I made a try at shaving, coughed up my morning ration of blood, and worked into a fresh nightshirt before she appeared. She had her hair put up and was wearing a green wool dress. Her smile made me feel like I wanted to live, but her eyes showed worry.

"Oh, Bud." She bent across the bed and kissed me, not even glancing back to see if anyone was watching through the open door. "Oh, I'm sorry. Did that hurt?"

It did, but I wasn't inclined to complain. "Terrible," I said. "Do it again."

This time her smile was better. "Bud! Here I've been fretted sick about you, and you tease me."

"You look good enough to eat," I answered, reaching out for her—carefully. "Anyway, there's nothing wrong with my ears. Visitors only talk that loud to folks about to die."

"Bud!" she protested again, but she leaned down for another kiss.

Looking past her, I noticed the new deputy standing in the middle of the parlor. With a star gleaming on his vest and a big pistol on his hip, he didn't look much like Milner's clerk. He had his hat in his hands, and he was staring at the floor, trying hard not to watch us through the doorway. Keeping my eyes on Braden, I pulled Ann close to me. My back felt like a bobcat was digging his burrow alongside my spine, but I held Annette until Braden met my challenging stare. His cheeks flushed, and he turned his back abruptly.

"My," Annette breathed when I let her go. "You can't be hurt too much." Then she saw where I was looking and went almost as red as the deputy had. "Oh, I've forgotten my manners! Bud, do you know Stone Braden, Papa's new deputy?"

My lip had cracked open again where Mayfield had butted me. I dabbed at the blood. "We've met," I said. Braden didn't say anything.

"Have you?" She glanced at him uncertainly, then back at me. "I didn't know—"

"At Milner's store," I said.

"Oh." She looked at Braden again. "Then—were you there when Bud was—hurt?"

"No. I was out with the wagon, making a delivery."

Until he denied it, I would've said the same thing. Then I began to wonder. He hadn't been around when I'd first entered the store, but it seemed to me I'd seen him in the crowd just before Mayfield had shot me. Still, Braden didn't have any reason to lie. Usually I'll figure a man's all right until he proves otherwise, but I hadn't found anything yet to like about Stone Braden.

Annette put her hand on mine. "I'd better go," she said. "I'm so glad you're better."

"You just got here."

"I'll come back tomorrow." Ann made a face at me. "You need somebody to look after you."

I didn't like that, not with Braden there. "I can look after myself," I growled.

"And a fine job you're doing, too! Just look where you are now."

"I made a mistake," I said. "Next time—" I stopped, realizing what I'd been about to say. *Next time I won't give somebody that chance.* But there wasn't going to be a next time, not ever again.

Ann was still looking at me. So was Braden.

"Next time I'll let you look after me," I finished. "I've already offered you the job."

Ann's cheeks flushed again, and she glanced quickly at the deputy. "We'll talk about that later," she told me. "Now don't you worry. You just rest and get well."

I didn't want to rest, but I didn't want to say any more with Braden there either. "Tomorrow, then," I said. Annette gave me a smile full of promises, then took Braden's arm. A draft of cold air swirled through the room as they left by the front door. For a minute I could hear them talking outside, and then they were gone.

Ma came in with a bowl of thick vegetable soup. "Since you didn't eat breakfast. Isn't it lucky the sheriff found someone like that to look after Annette?"

What I thought about luck wasn't fit to say in front of a lady. "If you like him so much, you should've offered him a cup of your coffee," I growled.

Ma's eyes were shrewd as a horse trader's. "It was good for you to see Annette," she said. "Your color's better already."

Probably I needed rest more than I thought, because I slept away the next week. Ann came to visit, but not as often as I would've liked, and always with Stone Braden. After the first time he waited outside, or had coffee in the kitchen, which was fine with me. A time or two Ann hinted that he might like to come in—I doubted that—but I never took up the hint. Some of my other friends dropped by now and then, too, but the time moved awful slow. Pa didn't say much, but often as not I'd wake to find him in my room, dozing in the deep armchair in the corner or reading a book by the light of the coal-oil lamp.

"Didn't mean to wake you, Bud," he'd say with a sheepish smile. "Just felt restless. Anything you need?"

By the time Sheriff Stanton came to call I was getting stronger every day and eager to be up and around, in spite of Doc Wisenhunt's warnings. I was sitting on the edge of the bed when Pa brought the sheriff in.

"Good to see you're doing well, Bud," he said. "I've been meaning to stop by. I guess Henry here has told you what kind of a story's going around about your shooting Mayfield."

I looked at Pa. He cleared his throat and studied the pattern in the rug. "Fact is, I hadn't thought to mention it, Amos." He frowned at the sheriff. "It doesn't do much good to repeat gossip."

"Saloon talk," I said. "That'd be Crabtree and his friends. What lie are they telling?"

Amos Stanton tugged at his mustache. "Well, they say Mayfield was the other man at the Wells—the one who shot at you."

"Was he?"

"It's likely. Doc says he had a fresh scar along the meat on his ribs, about where you might have nicked him."

I tried to put Mayfield at the Wells, slumped over with his head on his arms. It didn't seem right, but I hadn't seen much more than a shadow in the firelight that first time. Then there had been Davy and the ax swinging—

"Bud!"

I opened my eyes. My hands were clenched tight around the edge of the bedsprings, and I tasted blood at the back of my throat. "What else?" I demanded roughly. It came to me what the answer must be. "Anybody calling it murder?"

"No, not that." Stanton hesitated. "Not exactly," he added carefully. "Some of the witnesses thought you turned your back to Mayfield on purpose, to tempt him to draw."

"Draw what? I had his pistol in my hand! And why would I tempt him—so I could get my gizzard shot out?"

"So you'd have an excuse to kill him."

"And you believe something that crazy?"

The sheriff looked startled. "Why, hold on, Bud. I haven't said that."

No, he hadn't said it. He'd just hired Stone Braden to follow Annette around. Maybe part of Braden's job was to keep Annette away from me and the reputation I was getting.

"Was there a price on Mayfield?" I asked.

"Price?"

"It's your word. Reward. Is he worth anything dead?"

"Bud!" Pa gripped my shoulder. "You don't mean that!"

I shook his hand off. "Like hell I don't! I figure Mayfield owes me something. Whatever he's worth, I've earned it." I looked at the sheriff. "Well?"

"There's a reward, Bud. Three or four hundred dollars, maybe. I'll put in a claim for it if you say so."

"I say so. That's a season's hard work for a farmer."

"All right." The sheriff's face was expressionless. "I'd better remind you, those piney-woods folks stick together. I've arranged protection for Annette, in case anybody thinks to get at you that way. Best you be on your guard for a while." He turned toward the door. "I better get back to work. Thanks, Henry, but I'll see myself out."

"Bud, look at me," Pa said as soon as the sheriff had gone. "Why did you talk that way to Amos? You know you didn't mean it."

"I did." I met his eyes stubbornly. He was studying at me a little the way the cedar cutters had—like I was a rabid wolf. My back hurt, and a slow, burning ache was spreading through my chest. I eased myself back on the bed. "Pa? Do something for me, please."

"What, son?"

"My rifle's still at the gunsmith's. Get it for me." I reached out and patted the wall beside the bed. "I want it. Right here."

After Pa left I lay alone for what seemed a long time. I was sore and feverish, not nearly as spry as I had been a while before. There was a lot to think about—mostly about a town that would watch while I was shot down, then invent stories about it later. Even Sheriff Stanton sounded like he half believed Crabtree's version, and Pa was angry and ashamed for the way I'd acted toward the sheriff. I'd always trusted people pretty freely, but I was starting to learn better.

The way I felt, I didn't need any more visitors, but I got another one anyway. Ma tapped on the door, then stuck her head in to peer at me.

"I don't know," she whispered back over her shoulder. "I think he's asleep."

"I'm awake," I said. "What is it?"

"Oh, Bud, you startled me. You don't sound like yourself." She swung the door open a little wider. "If you don't feel like talking—I thought—Johnnie MacNally's here."

"Johnnie?" I worked myself up against the headboard so I was sitting again, concentrating on not showing Ma how much it hurt to move. "Sure. Let her come in."

Ma ushered her in, then went back to her sewing, pointedly leaving the door open into the parlor. Johnnie had a good-sized box in her arms, and she leaned around it to look at me.

"Hello, Bud. How are you?"

"Just dandy," I growled. Then I caught myself. Nothing that had happened was Johnnie's fault. "I'm all right. How's everyone out at your place?"

"Well—we're fine."

She sounded like she'd thought of saying something else. Looking close, I could see a cloud of worry in her eyes. Before I could ask what the matter was, though, she smiled and plunked the box down on the floor beside the bed.

"Here," she whispered with a glance at the doorway. "I brought them."

"Brought what?"

"*You* know. From your place."

I didn't know. "I hope it's my gun," I blurted. It surprised me as much as it did her, but it was true. That silver Colt would have been a lot of comfort to me just then.

"No, silly," Johnnie said after a moment. She came closer. "It's your cakes. The fruitcakes we were going to bake. I finished them and wrapped them up for you, but I wasn't sure of the names."

As she said it I could smell the spices. It seemed like something that had happened years ago. A lot of things had changed on account of Mayfield's bullet.

"Since it's so close to Christmas, I thought I'd better bring them," she was saying. "If you don't feel like—"

"I don't feel like anything." My voice was as low as a wolf's growl. "Fruitcakes! Something a kid would do. It was a stupid idea."

Johnnie backed a step away. "I thought it was a sweet idea," she said.

"Well, you're a kid yourself."

"I'm not!"

Johnnie pressed her lips together hard and stared at me. Tears from her dark eyes rolled down her cheeks. She scrubbed at them angrily with the back of a sun-browned hand.

"Damn you, Bud Tilden," she said, and then she whirled and ran out of the room. I heard the front door bang behind her.

"Johnnie!" I yelled. It hurt me all over, but I didn't stop. "Come back here! Don't leave these damn cakes here!"

I don't know if she heard me. Ma did. She was in the room like a shot.

"Henry Tilden Junior, you get right back in that bed. What's the matter with you? Fever's not any excuse to act that way!"

Without realizing it, I'd gotten to my feet. I dropped back on the bed like a worn-out coyote. Ma tucked me under the covers, scolding the whole time. In the doorway, Pa stood watching us like he didn't have any real family anywhere in the world.

"You ought to be ashamed of yourself," Ma finished. "I don't know what got into—why, what's this?" She bent over the box and took out a neatly wrapped fruitcake, and then another. "Why, I declare. I don't know why she brought so many, but it was sweet. Just look at all this candied fruit. She must have spent a fortune."

I hadn't thought of that, but now I remembered. I'd gone into town in the first place to buy the things on her list. My run-in with Mayfield had stopped me before I finished. That meant she'd used her own money and her own time baking those cakes. I started to say something about how sorry I was, forgetting she wasn't there. But then the scent of the spices in the room got so strong that I felt dizzy, and everything gradually faded out.

Chapter 7

MY FEVER BROKE FOR GOOD on Christmas Eve. Ma celebrated by feeding me up on a meal of steak and slabs of potato fried with onions, topped off by an apple cobbler. On Christmas Day Annette came to supper and stayed most of the evening. Since the weather was mild, I allowed that I felt good enough for a walk. We ended up on the old porch swing together.

"Didn't bring your bodyguard today?" I asked.

"I should have. You're getting healthy too fast. Stop that, now." She pulled back and looked at me seriously. "Bud, I wish you'd get to know Stone better. I'm sure you two would like each other."

"I'm sure."

"Really! He was so quiet at first, kind of drawn inside himself. I thought he was just unsociable. But underneath, he's nice—quiet and gentle, the way you—are."

"Thanks." I had the feeling she'd almost ended her

sentence another way. "Is there some reason we have to talk about Stone Braden right now?"

Annette smiled at me. "No, Bud. Not if you don't want to." She touched my arm. "I just thought—"

"Well, I don't." I stood up and went to the edge of the porch, leaning on the worn wooden railing. It needed fixing. Splinters dug into my palms when I closed my hands on it. "It's time we went inside," I said.

Before she left that night she gave me my present—a new flannel shirt she'd sewn herself. I gave her a fruitcake.

I didn't get my last Christmas wish until a few days later. Even then my folks weren't happy about the idea.

"I hate to see you out there by yourself," Ma said. "You're still not over being shot. What if it comes a norther?"

"I'll manage." Truth was, I'd had about as much coddling as I could stand. "It's time I got home."

Will Stanton volunteered to drive my wagon out to the farm—mostly to get a day off from school, I figured. I loaded my Christmas plunder and said my good-byes, and finally we got on our way. Like a lot of December days, this one was warm and fair. We shed our coats before we were out of town good. Feeling the sharp breeze on my face made me feel better than I had in weeks, but a quiet, steady ache in my ribs reminded me the roadside might hold more than blue jays and flocks of sparrows. My rifle was leaning against my knee, and I put out my hand to touch it. Will saw me.

"I thought we might get a buck," I said.

Will gave me a knowing smile. "Aw, you can tell me the truth." He hesitated a second, then added, "Papa's pretty sure that Mayfield feller you killed was the one at the Wells. That makes two."

"Two?"

"Two outlaws. You know, Papa's been a lawman 'most twenty years, and he hasn't ever killed anybody."

I hadn't known that. Before I had time to think about it Will was talking again.

"Stone don't carry a rifle. Don't guess he needs one much in town." He cocked an eye at me. "He's got his own handgun, though—an old army cap and ball that belonged to his pa. It's not near as nice as yours." He paused again. "He let me clean it last week."

"Did he?"

The road curved downhill through a field of dead sunflowers, putting us out of sight of town. I looked at them and thought about Braden's pa.

"Where does Braden say he comes from?"

"He never said. Gave Papa a letter, though, says he's from a good family in Tennessee. They're all dead now, I guess."

At the foot of the hill I looked north along the creek. The tin roof of Josh Ledbetter's barn gleamed in the morning sun beside a stand of dark green live oaks. Next to the barn a paint horse lifted its head to watch us pass.

"Got his own horse, too," Will said. "Little chestnut gelding with two white stockings. Stone let me curry him last week."

"I'll bet he'd even let you whitewash his fence."

From Will's puzzled look I figured he hadn't come to *Tom Sawyer* in his reading yet. "He ain't even got a fence," he said. "He sure asks a bunch of questions about you, though. I guess he must like you a lot."

"Oh?" If Stone Braden had any special liking for

me, he'd surely kept it hidden. "What kind of questions?"

"Oh, just regular stuff. That's about all him and Annette ever talk about, when—" He stopped all at once, then finished more slowly. "When they're together. That's what Annette says."

"Sounds like they're pretty thick, Braden and Annette."

Will tightened his grip on the lines and stared hard at the mule's rear end. "I wouldn't know," he said.

We rode for a while without talking, which was all right with me. I wanted to soak up about three weeks' worth of rocks and trees and thin high clouds with pale blue sky at the western horizon. We came to the deeper blue water in Ted Willowby's reservoir, the only pond in the county that never went dry. Three wood ducks bobbed up and down close to the far bank. I watched them as we went by, thinking to myself the Lord had been in a good mood when he'd put this day together.

We were easing up the last hill toward my place before Will spoke again. "I hope everything's the way you left it, Bud," he said. "I tried to keep things in good shape for you."

Judging by my first sight of the farm, he'd done a good job. The mules in the low pasture felt frisky enough to take off running as soon as they saw the wagon. Somebody had replaced the broken fence post I'd been meaning to get around to, and it looked like I hadn't lost any chickens.

"I'd say you did fine, Will. I'm obliged."

"Best part's in the barn." He stopped the wagon right by the porch. "You go on inside, though. I'll bring your parcels up when I come."

I'd been thinking I'd rather see the barn, but the ache in my side was more than an annoyance after the bouncing of the wagon. I took my rifle and climbed down slowly, feeling like an old man. I was surprised to see Will had swept the porch, and even more surprised at what I found when I stepped through the door.

Usually, a place that's been empty has a cold, deserted smell, musty and lonesome as the grave. That's how I'd expected the cabin to be. Instead, the whole house was warm and pleasant from a fire in the grate. The floor was swept clean enough to eat on. All the litter I'd left behind was cleared away, and every dish in the place was washed and on the shelf. Coffee perked on the stove. It was like I'd never been away, only a lot tidier than I'd ever have kept it. For a minute I just stood there and stared.

"Surprise!"

The shout came from behind me. I was halfway around before I was able to stop, working the lever of my Winchester to put a shell into the chamber. Then my mind took over again, and I managed to keep the rifle pointed upward while I lowered the hammer to half cock. Annette had been waiting behind the door. She was staring at me like a startled doe.

"I—Bud." She stopped and swallowed. "Welcome home." She made a good try at a smile. "I didn't mean to scare you."

"Ann!"

Putting the rifle aside, I caught her in my arms. I wanted to explain, but I couldn't. There was no way to explain about my dreams during the fever, dreams where a man I didn't know always laughed at me. Sometimes he was with Annette. Sometimes he was cocking a pistol aimed at me. His blank face would usually melt into Stone Braden's, and I'd wake up still hearing his laughter.

"Ann," I said again, burying my face in the softness

of her hair. My fever was gone now. I was home, and Ann was real. I lifted her face and gave her the deepest, hungriest kiss a woman ever lived through. She clung to me for a long time, but not near long enough. Finally she pried herself away and pointed out the window.

"Will," she gasped.

Sure enough, he was tromping across the yard from the barn. I swung Annette around like we were dancing. Leaning solidly against the door, I kissed her until Will got tired of hammering and shouting. Finally Ann kicked me on the shin harder than anybody ought to kick a person who's just gotten over being shot. I went to see about the coffee, leaving her to explain to Will why he hadn't been able to get in.

"—sick and tired of it!" he was saying when I came back. "Every time lately when I try to come in where you are—"

"Will!" Annette looked quickly at me, then away. "Just hush," she said.

It came to me that any situation in the world could be ruined by a girl's kid brother. "Coffee's ready," I said. There was no profit in following the trail Will had started down, so I thanked them both for fixing the place up.

"You're a good man," I told Will, and he looked proud as a puppy with an old shoe.

"Aw, it wasn't much," he said, sipping his coffee and trying not to make a face. "All the kids from school wanted to come out and see your place—'specially your silver Colt—but I wouldn't let them."

"Yes," Ann said, looking at me over the rim of her cup. "You're still their hero."

"I told you before, I'm nobody's hero."

But she only smiled. "Mine," she said.

In the end we had a meal together around my little

kitchen table. Ann had fixed a roast and biscuits and potatoes, with an apricot pie she'd probably brought from home. I washed the dishes and she dried them, and then we sneaked down to the barn together while Will was dozing in the front room.

We were both remembering that time we'd been together in Hart's stable, and it was like Stone Braden hadn't ever existed. I think Ann would have gone to the loft with me right then, except that my back and ribs weren't going to let me climb any ladders. It was something else Mayfield's bullet had spoiled, but at least we had a few minutes together before it was time to hitch up her buggy.

I stood on the porch and watched Ann and Will drive out of sight. All at once the place seemed so lonely that I couldn't see how I'd ever been happy there by myself.

For a couple of months things just kind of ran along. New Year's came, and it was 1882. A jury up north finally decided the fellow who'd shot President Garfield was sane enough to hang. The Willis gang got into a shooting scrape with some federal marshals up in Indian Territory, and most folks thought they'd ducked down into Texas to hide out. Annette didn't need guarding any more, now that the gunfighting scare had died down, so Stone Braden went to work at regular deputy chores, the sort of thing Davy had done.

Around the farm, I could barely keep up. I'd pretty well had my winter plowing done and my equipment laid by before I was shot—a good thing, too, because I didn't feel like doing much. I put off planting corn and potatoes until the almanac said it was too late—not that it mattered, because the reward money I was expecting for Mayfield would more than make up the difference. My chest still pained me some. More than that, the farm seemed awful lonely, something I'd never noticed before.

Every chance I got I'd run into town to see Annette, or just to visit at Milner's store or the barber shop. I'd noticed that people paid more attention to my opinion on things, even Judge Poe. The one person in town who didn't seem impressed was Stone Braden.

I was just walking out of Milner's store one day when I plowed right into him—it seemed like the Lord had put him on earth just to run into me in doorways. He didn't drop anything this time, but he did step back fast and put a hand to that big pistol he carried. I held my hands out by my sides to show I wasn't armed.

"Nervous, Deputy?" I asked.

"Not over you." He didn't sound too friendly. Come to think of it, neither did I.

"My mistake." Since he was out of the doorway, I came through it. "You ought to give some warning where you're going. Even a sidewinder rattles before it strikes."

Like always, there were several people in the store—two or three women shopping and a few men sitting and chewing and swapping lies. Braden glanced past me to see if any of them had overheard.

"Listen, Tilden," he began, his voice quiet and cold.

"Hey, Stone," Todd Milner called from the back of the store. "Come on out to the storage barn. We're just ready to uncrate it."

Braden's eyes moved that way, then flicked back to me. "I'll see you later," he promised.

"I can't wait."

He brushed past me, then turned. "I figured you'd be at the sheriff's office by now," he said. "Your blood money's come."

"You mean the reward?"

"You heard me."

"I don't much care for the way you put that."

"Maybe you—"

Todd yelled again, impatient this time. "Stone, come *on!* I've got other customers, too."

Without another word Braden turned his back on me and strode toward the back door. I watched him for a minute. "Bad blood there," I heard a woman murmur, but when I looked around everybody was awfully involved in his own business. While I was standing there it came to me why I hadn't liked Braden's remark about blood money. Those were the words I'd used about the reward for killing Trey Bonner.

When I finished my errands and got down to the sheriff's office I was glad to learn Sheriff Stanton didn't feel that way about it at all. If he remembered how I'd behaved when I told him to claim the reward, he'd long since forgiven me.

"Just take this draft over to the bank and they'll cash it for you," he said with a smile. "Right at five hundred dollars. Not much for a high roller, maybe, but a lot of hard money for a working man. What do you propose to do with it?"

I'd already planned what I was going to say, but I felt myself stumbling a little anyway.

"I figure to put some of it into fixing up the place, and some into breeding stock—horses." I swallowed, then plowed on through. "I thought I might use the rest for a honeymoon trip—if I had your permission."

The sheriff smiled in a different way as he eyed me. He didn't seem surprised. "In this modern world, some young men wouldn't ask my consent," he said.

"I'm asking."

He tugged at his mustache, taking longer than I liked with his answer. "I won't speak for Annette," he said finally. "It's her life and her choice—but you can give her the chance to decide."

I grinned at him. "She won't have long to wait," I said.

"Bud, she's—" he began, but I was already on my way. Outside, I headed straight for the Stanton home. The sun seemed brighter than it had when I'd gone into the office. The day was cold enough that I was bundled in my coat, but I felt warm inside. Greeting the townsfolk along the street, I liked them every one—especially the children toddling along with their parents. All the best things in life lay just ahead for me and Annette.

A shiny black buggy came around a corner, pulled by a proud chestnut. I paused to admire the rig and the horse, then glanced at the passengers. Annette sat beside the driver, wrapped in a green wool coat and scarf, her hands hidden in a brown fur muff. When she saw me she pulled a hand free and waved gaily, but the driver's eyes met mine with a flat glare, and this time the challenge was all his. As I stepped back from the mud splashed up by the high red wheels I was a little surprised that the deputy's job paid enough for Stone Braden to order a new buggy.

I cashed my draft at the bank and headed back out to the farm. Toward dusk, I put a pot of coffee on to boil, then took my silver Colt out of its box. I sat holding it for a long time while light died out of the sky outside. Finally I put it away and went to fix supper, thinking that I really ought to find myself a holster sometime soon.

Chapter 8

THAT NEXT WEEK a blue norther came through and left the ground white with sleet. The weather was too cold for doing more than everyday chores, so I fell to working with my new pistol. I'd wished for it when I was laid up; now I had time to toy with it. I learned every piece from taking it apart and loading and unloading it and giving it needless cleanings. It still felt good in my hand, but when I first came to use it I found out how much I didn't know.

Though I'd grown up shooting a rifle, I'd never had much to do with handguns. At first I tried to aim the Colt like it was my carbine, holding it at arm's length and sighting along the barrel. The gun seemed to twist in my hand like a snake. The trigger tightened up faster than I expected, and the Colt roared. Bark flew from the tree trunk a yard above my mark. My next two shots didn't even hit the tree.

I was almighty disgusted, ready to go back to the house and put the Colt away for good. As I turned I caught sight of an old paint can I'd left hanging from a fence post. Without thinking I lifted the gun, letting the hammer drop as my arm came level. There was a clang, and the can spun around the post like a dust devil. The muzzle followed it as naturally as a finger pointing. Another bullet lifted it off the post. The last round in the chamber kicked it far out into the weeds.

After that I had the idea. The smooth ivory handle felt right in my hand again. I worked with the gun every day, using up enough cartridges for a winter's hunting. Finally I hammered some scrap lumber into a target that was five feet high and roughly man-shaped. On the first really warm day of March I dragged it out into the pasture and paced off thirty yards.

The first six shots went firm and true. Laughing, I punched the spent casings out of the cylinder and reloaded. Then I turned on my man-target, firing as fast as I could thumb back the hammer. When the gun clicked empty there was nothing but splintered wood where the target's heart had been.

I was loading the Colt again when I heard the pasture gate creak open behind me. I spun around, startled. Johnnie MacNally stood there, holding the reins of her horse. I swore at myself for not hearing her ride up.

"Is it safe?" she called, looking like she really wasn't sure.

I realized I was holding the pistol ready—not pointed at her, but ready. Lowering it, I forced a laugh.

"You're about the last person on earth I'd shoot, Johnnie. Come on up."

She swung the gate closed and dropped the reins, letting the horse nose around in the dry grass. She was looking at the ragged hole in the target.

"I heard shooting. Shouldn't you pick on somebody your own size?"

"Maybe." I finished loading the pistol and stuck it in my belt the way Mayfield had carried his. "Listen, I meant to thank you for baking those cakes for me."

"It's all right."

"I'm sorry about the way I acted. I was—"

"It's all right," she repeated. "Todd Milner said you paid off what I owed at the store. We're even."

I didn't press it. Being even was probably the best I was going to do.

"Well, do you want to—"

"What I came to talk about was Luke. He's gone off someplace with that saloon trash he runs with."

"That'd be the two men he was with at Finster's?" I asked.

Johnnie nodded. Her face had that same look she'd worn when she saw me with the rum bottle. "They were hanging around, trying to talk Luke into something, I think. Then one day they were gone, and Luke, too. Matthew's out looking for him."

"What's Matthew mean to do when he finds him?"

Johnnie looked at me. "Bring him back," she said simply.

It occurred to me that Luke was going to get pretty tired of being dragged home across brother Matthew's shoulder. Maybe he'd already gotten tired of it and was trying to prove he was a man. I'd never cared much for Luke, but I could see how growing up among the MacNallys might explain some of his ways.

"I wanted you to know," Johnnie said. "Just in case . . ." She paused like she wasn't quite sure how to finish, and then she shrugged. "Just in case."

She looked so unhappy standing there that I was tempted to put my arms around her to comfort her. I didn't know how she'd react to that. Come to think of it, I didn't know how I'd react, either, so I said, "Johnnie, if there's anything I can do, tell me."

"Thanks." Then she pressed her lips together and looked hard at the target I'd made. "You're a good shot." It sounded like a compliment, but there was no admiration in the way she said it. "Like Matthew."

"Just trying out the gun. It doesn't mean anything."

"Bud, it does." Johnnie's voice was serious now. "I've watched Matthew practice. I know what it means to him—living or dying, sometimes. Just because you can shoot holes in a board—"

I turned away, swallowing through a tight throat. "I know what it's like," I reminded her harshly.

Out across the pasture a big red-tailed hawk was quartering the ground for mice. He must have seen some movement, because one of his wings dipped, and he turned sharply toward us, spiraling down to within ten feet of the ground.

"Bud, I'm—" Johnnie began.

I don't know what made me do it. It was like the silver Colt was thinking for me—or maybe it was a moment's vision of Mayfield's beaked face, eyes as bright and emotionless as the hawk's. The Colt was in my hand, sweeping up, hammer rocking back as the hawk screeched and began an upward swoop—

"Bud, don't!"

The Colt roared.

Whatever I had thought, I'd never had any idea of hitting the bird. That first bullet, though, shattered one of the stiff wings and spun the hawk the way my practice shot had spun the paint can. The second bullet hit in a spray of blood and feathers, and the third ripped the tumbling mess, no longer a bird, almost to pieces.

I lowered the gun, almost as shocked at what I'd done as Johnnie. Her face was deadly pale, a dusting of freckles that I'd never noticed before standing out like scars across the bridge of her nose. I gripped the Colt tight, hardly noticing the barrel was burning my left hand. I expected her face to show the expression I was getting accustomed to, the one that said I was some kind of wild animal. Instead, she looked at me with a deep, abiding sadness.

"Johnnie," I began, and I had to swallow back a sudden sickness. "Johnnie, I didn't mean . . ."

I stopped, because her eyes had shifted past me. Her face changed all at once. She seemed harder, and her clear eyes were hooded, hiding her feelings. I turned around to see a rider on the hillside, sitting silent and motionless as a figure in a dream. He'd stopped sideways to us, his face shadowed, one hand holding the reins and the other on his hip. I realized first that he'd come across the fields instead of following the road, and second that he wore a brass badge pinned on his coat. Then I recognized him: Stone Braden. Even from where I stood I could see his right hand was resting on his holster.

For all of a minute, nobody moved. Then Braden kicked his horse into motion and came toward us. He looked from me to the hawk and back again. His face didn't show anything, but he moved his hand away from his pistol.

"Tilden." He tipped his hat to Johnnie. "Morning, Miss MacNally."

"Hello," Johnnie said. I didn't say anything.

Braden sat back in his saddle. "Looks like you've been practicing," he said with another glance toward the hawk.

Up until then I hadn't been able to think of anything except him and Annette together in his buggy. I shook the idea off, but probably I still didn't sound glad to see him.

"I guess you got lost," I told him politely. "Around here, most folks come along the road, unless they're up to something underhanded." Watching his face, I grinned. "Of course, some people just prefer to do things behind somebody's back."

Braden's cheeks colored, but he didn't answer directly. "I didn't come to visit," he said. "Sheriff Stanton sent me. I was coming out to your place, too, Miss MacNally. I wanted to talk to your brother Matt."

Johnnie lowered her eyes. "He's—away." She turned from him to speak to me. "I was just going. Goodbye, Bud."

"Wait, Johnnie," I said. "It's all right."

"Sure enough, Miss MacNally." Braden smiled a tight little smile at me. "I just needed to talk to Bud here a minute. I didn't mean to interrupt anything."

There wasn't a good answer to that, so I didn't bother. "What's your business, Deputy?"

He stopped smiling. "The sheriff's getting up a posse. He—some of the folks in town—Sheriff Stanton said to ask if Matt MacNally would join up. He said to ask you, too, since it was on my way."

I stared at him. There hadn't been a posse mounted out of Comanche for almost as long as I could remember—not since the day Wes Hardin shot a Brown County officer in Comanche when I was about twelve years old. The last I'd heard, Hardin was safe in prison, so he likely wasn't the problem this time.

"I wouldn't have come except the sheriff told me to," Braden added, evidently figuring my silence meant more than it did. "Ann—that is, I said you probably wouldn't feel up to riding yet."

Beside me, Johnnie stirred. Whatever she'd thought of, she didn't put it into words.

"Nice of you," I said to Braden. "What's the posse for?"

"Probably it's nothing," he said grudgingly. "Three men shot up a bank in Waco. Some of the witnesses said it was the Willis brothers. The sheriff thought they might come this way."

"There's a lot of country between here and Waco."

Braden shrugged. "Like I said, probably nothing." He started to rein his horse around. "I'll tell them you can't make it."

"Hold on."

He looked at me, then at the bloodstained heap of feathers that had been the hawk. He couldn't seem to keep his eyes away from it.

"It's dangerous work," he said. "Hard riding, too, for a dollar a day. Probably it wasn't even the Willises, so you wouldn't collect any reward this time."

He was wearing that little smile again. He didn't seem to like me a bit better than I liked him—but, remembering him with Ann, I knew what my reason was. Also, what he'd said was true as gospel; I had no business riding around the country trying to get myself shot again. I thought about that, then thought about mashing his smile against his teeth.

"I'll go," I told him. "You might not know, just drifting through, but around here, neighbors help each other when there's trouble."

"So I noticed. I guess Miss MacNally was in plenty of trouble when I rode up—and you were just getting set to help her."

I'll admit I'd been trying to get his goat, but he'd gotten mine instead. I took a step forward, the only idea in my mind being to pull him down off that horse. I stopped when Johnnie's fingers bit deep into my arm.

"Bud! No!"

She had both hands on my right wrist. Her nails had

brought blood where they'd dug into the skin. That was when I realized I'd reached up for Braden only with my left hand. The fingers of my right were clenched around the butt of the silver Colt.

Braden reined his mount smartly back a step or two. He'd been startled, but in a second his smile was back. "You're pretty quick to reach for that gun, Tilden," he said. "Maybe your nerves aren't strong enough for a manhunt."

I didn't get over it as fast. All of a sudden I was realizing what might have happened if Johnnie hadn't been there. Worse, I knew that Braden was right; I'd gone for the Colt without even thinking about it—just like with the hawk.

I glared at Braden, keeping my voice as steady as I could. "You've had your say, friend. Ride out—by the gate this time. Tell the sheriff I'll be there as soon as I get my gear together."

Braden laughed. "I'll tell him." He touched his heels to the chestnut. "I know he'll be relieved, having a fast gun like you along to keep us safe. Nice seeing you, Miss MacNally."

I watched him through the gate and out of sight along the road before I turned back to Johnnie. She'd gone to stand beside her little roan.

"I'll go now, Bud." She wouldn't look at me, and I wondered what she was thinking. "We can talk about—what I came for—later, after you get back." She swung into the saddle, and then she did look at me, with the same expression in her clear blue eyes that she'd had when I killed the hawk—concerned and awfully sad.

"Be careful, Bud," she said. "Look out for yourself."

Then she was gone, down across the pasture and out the gate. Braden had left it open. She closed it.

For a minute or two I just stood there, getting the shakes out of my insides. Finally I walked to the house to get my gear. Just as I reached the porch I saw the rider, silhouetted on the ridge that Matthew had watched from when he was protecting Johnnie's honor. I thought it might be him, but the figure seemed slimmer and smaller than Matthew. It could have been Johnnie. She'd just about had time to get there. Before I could be sure, horse and rider dropped off the skyline, back across the ridge toward the MacNally place, leaving me with a final picture to think about. Whoever it was had been carrying a rifle, out of the scabbard and ready to use. I pushed on inside, but all of a sudden the farm didn't seem like the safe haven I'd always thought it was.

Besides Braden and me, Todd Milner from the store and Alf Cryer, the woodworker from Mr. Perry's hardware, finished out the posse. The sheriff was disappointed not to have Matthew MacNally along—so was I—but it wasn't enough to make him pick anyone else. Amos Stanton knew his men. Todd was a hunter, as good a rifle shot as we had in the county. Old Alf had ridden with Bedford Forrest in the war, then had hunted buffalo on the plains before settling down. His big single-boom Sharps might be as cumbersome as a cannon, but it would outrange anything except another like it. I knew I'd been picked because of my new reputation, and I figured I could live up to it. The only one I wasn't sure of was Braden.

The others had already gathered on the porch outside Sheriff Stanton's office by the time I rode in. I was surprised to see both Annette and Will Stanton there, Will perched on the hitch rail where he could see everything. Annette was inside the office, looking out through the window. She had on the green coat I'd seen before but still was hugging herself like she was cold. When she saw me she made a little anxious movement toward the door, then stopped. Her pa was talking to Tom Perry, Alf's boss from the hardware store.

"I appreciate it, Tom," the sheriff was saying. "I'd be glad to have you, but you'd have to close the store if you and Alf both came. And it's Alf we'll need." A smile twitched his mustache. "To make coffins for the Willis boys."

We laughed a little louder than the joke deserved. Mr. Perry was too crippled up to make the ride, but he seemed to feel it was a point of honor. The sheriff took time to smooth his feathers the way he did voters before election, until Mr. Perry felt mighty proud to be left in charge while the rest of us went hunting outlaws. Will Stanton, though, was harder to handle.

"You promised to take me along as soon as I was old enough," he said. "Well, I'm old enough now."

"There's school to consider, son."

"School's always there, but we don't hardly ever have a posse. Shoot, I'll have white hair and a long beard by the time I really learn anything about lawing."

"You planning to grow a beard, Will?"

Alf Cryer tugged his own white-streaked beard and laughed. Will's face went red. He jumped off the rail and stomped into the office. Braden said something quiet to the sheriff, and I heard Alf second it.

"Sure, Amos. We'll look after the young'un, if you've a mind to bring him along."

I was tying Reno at the rail. He was the one extravagant thing I owned, the best saddle horse I'd been able to buy. I stroked his neck as Sheriff Stanton looked a question at me. Knowing how much of a nuisance Will could be, I hesitated a second, but then

I remembered how hard he'd worked around the place when I was laid up.

"Fine with me," I said. The sheriff nodded, then went inside the office. He came out a moment later with his arm around Will's shoulders.

"I want you to bring the .32-20 Winchester with a box of shells," he said. "And you'd best get your heavy coat."

"You don't need my coat."

"I don't need your rifle, either, but you won't be much good to us without it."

Will blinked at him, figuring that out. Then he gave a delighted whoop and tore off down the street before his pa could change his mind. Sheriff Stanton shook his head again, smiling under his mustache.

"I'd better add a few things to our supplies," Todd said with a grin. "I've seen that kid eat."

"That's fine," Sheriff Stanton said. "Me and Alf will get our horses and meet you back here."

I glanced toward the office, thinking I might speak to Annette. Braden was just going inside. "Hey, Todd, wait up," I called. "I'll give you a hand."

Todd paused until I caught up, and we started off toward the store. We hadn't gone a dozen steps when the office door banged and I heard running footsteps behind us.

"Bud!" Annette's voice called. "Bud, wait!"

Todd turned back toward her. After another step I did, too. She stopped in front of me, flushed and out of breath. Stone Braden stood watching from the doorway of the office, his mouth pulled down in a scowl.

"Bud, I need to see you," Annette said.

"You see me. I'm on my way to help Todd with the supplies."

Todd pushed back his hat, looking from Annette to

me. "Reckon I can do by myself," he said. "Don't be late, Bud."

He swung on his way, whistling. Annette and I stood for a moment longer, things between us about as awkward as I could ever remember.

"Weren't you even going to speak to me before you left, Bud?" she asked.

"Didn't figure I was needed." I glanced toward Braden. "You seemed to have plenty of company."

She pressed her lips together without speaking. After a time she took my arm and tugged at it. "Walk with me, Bud, please," she said. "I have to talk to you."

"All right."

We walked up Main, away from the office and Braden. Annette didn't say anything at first, and neither did I. A cold wind was pushing along from the north, and she moved closer to me. Finally, she looked up into my face.

"Bud, you're wrong about Stone. He's not like you think." She waited, but I didn't answer. "Is that why you haven't been to visit? Because of him?"

I shrugged. "You'd been seeing so much of Braden, I didn't think you'd notice I was gone." I hadn't meant to sound so bitter, but once I was started, it just kept on. "I don't have a buggy to ride in, nor a steady job with your pa."

"You've got that MacNally girl for a neighbor, though," Annette said tartly. "From what I've heard, you haven't been lonely."

That caught me up short. I mentally cursed Braden, then realized it probably wasn't all his doing. Tales get carried one way or another, and the town talk obviously hadn't all been about my speed with a gun.

"There's nothing between Johnnie and me." As I

said it I suddenly wondered if it was true. "I don't know any reason why you should believe me."

"The same reason you should believe me about Stone. I love you." Annette's voice caught. "Bud, I don't want to fight with you. Just come on."

We had turned along a side street by the church. Hart's stable was just ahead. I realized suddenly that was where Annette had been leading me.

"Wait." I stopped, taking her hands. "I have to go," I said. "Your pa and the others are waiting."

Ann looked at me steadily. The pale winter sunlight brought out the green in her eyes.

"Is it so important?" she asked softly.

Just for that moment, it wasn't. More than anything in the world I wanted to turn my back on the posse and the name I'd made for myself and the silver Colt lying in my saddlebag. I wanted to forget it all and take Annette back to the loft, back before everything had started to go bad between us. Maybe that's what I should have done, but too many things had changed since then. I'd changed.

I took a step away from her, still holding her hands. "I promised," I said.

Annette put her arms around my waist, holding me tightly to her. "Bud," she said against my shoulder. "Bud, let's not wait. Let's get married right away—the minute you get back."

"Ann, do you mean that?"

"Oh, yes, Bud, please."

She was trembling against me. "I'll be all right, Ann," I said. "This posse business won't amount to anything but a couple of days riding around. We'll talk to Brother Winslow as soon as it's done with."

"I've been so mixed up!" Annette put her face up for a kiss, and I could taste the salt of her tears. "I wish it could be now—that you didn't have to leave."

"I do. Right now." I kissed her again quickly, not caring who saw. "Don't worry, Ann. Everything's just fine now."

She nodded as if she believed me, and I released her and started for the sheriff's office. When I looked back she was still standing where I'd left her, crying into the bunched collar of her green coat.

Chapter 9

WE FOLLOWED THE ROAD most of the way to the little community of Blanket before we swung off to the west. For an hour the horses rustled through belly-high dead grass. Then we left the farm country behind and broke into ridges and ravines so rocky that only the hardiest scrub brush could live there. From a couple of landmarks I knew the sheriff was leading us in a wide sweep that would probably bring us back across the emigrant road sometime toward nightfall.

Braden had gone ahead a little way to act as scout, and the rest of us stayed strung out behind the sheriff. I was staring at Reno's ears, trying to sort out what Annette had said, and why I wasn't as happy as I should have been that she wanted to get married right away. The others seemed to have their own thoughts. Even Will rode in silent concentration, studying each clump of brush as if the whole Willis gang might be holed up behind it. After a few miles Alf Cryer pulled up alongside me.

"Sure beats the old days," he said with a grin, patting his sides with both hands. Thin and wiry, he was huddled inside a blanket coat that would have held two of him. He'd tied a plain red scarf over his head and ears with his hat stuffed down over it.

"A man can go a long way with a warm coat and a good horse under him," he added. "Even riding in circles the way we're doing." He ran his eyes over Reno's lines. "That's a nice-looking mount you've got there."

Alf's horse was a tall gray stallion with a lot of speed and spirit. Reno was smaller and closer-coupled, but I figured he could give the gray a good race. I didn't say so. Alf liked good horseflesh and liked everybody else to notice. I complimented the gray, then said, "I've been thinking the same thing about the circles. What do you think the sheriff's doing?"

"Oh, Amos knows his onions. I figure he's just checking the game trails to see if anybody's passed this way. If I can still read directions, we'll be back along the road in time to camp for the night." He gestured toward my middle. "You should've brought that silver pistol along. If we find them Willises, you're like to need it."

I didn't mean to get within six-gun range of the Willis brothers if I could help it, but I didn't say so. "The Colt's in my saddlebag," I said. "I don't have a belt for it yet."

"Won't do you a lick of good in a saddlebag. You ought to tuck it in the top of your boot, the way we did in Old Bedford's horse cavalry. Your pa must have showed you."

I laughed. "Not likely. Pa doesn't hold much with handguns. I don't expect he even knows how to shoot one."

"Well, I'll swear!" Alf looked at me strangely. "I'd

just expect he does—leastwise, unless he's forgot an awful lot since '64. Hasn't he ever told you anything about those times?"

That was enough to take my mind off Annette. "About the war, you mean? Not much. Did you know him then?"

"Why, I reckon I did! Him and me rode many a mile together, just like we're doing now—'cept the horses was leaner and I didn't have me a coat." He grinned fiercely. "I was just a young'un, but Henry had been with Forrest near two years. He wore a pair of Navy Colts he'd took off a Yank major . . ."

Alf stopped all at once, eyeing me.

"Go on," I said. I'd heard a lot of his stories of the war and the plains when I was younger—tall tales, I'd figured—but he'd never mentioned Pa before. "What about him?"

"No." Alf shook his head slowly. "If it was his idea not to tell you, it ain't fitting that I should. But I can sure understand why he wouldn't want you living by the gun."

I tried to press him, but he raised up in his stirrups and pointed ahead. "There, I told you Amos was leading us back to the road. Reckon he had this planned all along. We couldn't ask for a better place to camp than the Wells."

While we'd talked, the afternoon had gotten along. The sun was right ahead of us, laced across with bare branches from the trees around the Wells. No matter what Alf said, I'd rather have camped anywhere else in the world, but Sheriff Stanton plainly meant to stop. He was leading us toward a campsite down to the south, where Braden already had a fire going. The trail took us right by the place Davy had been killed. I couldn't help reining up for a second.

Winter rains had washed out the blood of that November evening. The smell of burned leather was long blown away by the wind. The bloodstained tree the Mennonite had shown me was just another oak, and only a blackened ring of stones marked where the cedar cutters had given me my first drink of whiskey. Except for us, the whole place was deserted. It was no season for traveling.

"Right there's where it happened, huh?" Alf's harsh voice pulled me back from my thoughts.

"Yeah. That's where it happened."

"Terrible thing. I don't think I'll ever forget that night you brought him in. Reckon you won't either."

Without thinking about it I slid my hand down to touch the worn stock of my carbine. "I reckon," I said.

By the time we'd unsaddled and set the horses out to graze, Will Stanton was off in the brush with his little rifle. Todd got busy cooking up a meal. I pitched in to help, though what I wanted most was to lie down on my bedroll and never move again. I'd thought I was over the effects of Mayfield's bullet, but those slow hours in the saddle had taught me better. My legs and back ached from the strain, and my insides felt like my gizzard had jarred loose from my backbone.

Braden made himself useful around camp, but without ever settling down to one job. Next time I really noticed him, he was leaning against a tree watching me from under his hat brim. I'd just met his eyes when a shot from Will's .32-20 cracked out behind me.

Braden jumped. I guess I did, too. The sheriff put down the canvas water pail he'd been carrying and straightened angrily. "I should've stopped that before it started," he muttered. "Will!"

"No harm done, Amos," Cryer said. "We weren't apt to sneak up on anybody here."

Will came in wagging a dead rabbit by the ears.

"You killed it," his pa said. "You skin and clean it for supper."

Braden pushed himself away from the tree, still looking at me. "Here, I'll help," he said.

For a little while nobody had much to say. I got a chance to relax on the dry grass and ease some of the kinks in my back. Sheriff Stanton hunkered against a log to pack his pipe with tobacco. Except for Todd, who was doing the cooking, everybody seemed content just to sit; likely they were all as tired as me. Finally, when the stew was bubbling in the big camp kettle we'd packed along, Alf Cryer stretched himself and cocked an eye at the sheriff.

"Being as we've already broke silence," he said, "I'd admire to see Bud shoot his fancy Colt—if you don't mind, Amos."

Amos Stanton looked thoughtful. Then, to my surprise, he nodded. "I guess we've got enough light left," he said. "It'll give us something to do while the stew's cooking."

"Well, I don't know." For some reason, I didn't like the idea at all. "I didn't bring but one box of shells—"

"You use .44-40s, don't you?" Todd put in. "I've brought plenty. All on the county, right, Sheriff?"

"Let me shoot it!" Will cried. "I know how! You and Stone have both showed me."

"All right," I said quickly. Sheriff Stanton frowned a little, but I got the Colt from my saddlebag and emptied the cylinder before handing it to Will.

While he loaded it with the shells Todd gave him Alf set up four or five empty tins against the trunk of an oak. Will squared off at the target and let fly. The Colt bucked up smartly, carrying his arm with it. The shot struck the oak without doing the cans any damage.

"Gosh!" Will mumbled. His pa gave him a little

advice about aiming, and his third shot smashed one of the cans. He got two more with his three remaining shots, then shelled out the empties and gave the pistol back to me.

"Gosh, Bud, that's harder than it looks. Show me how you do it."

I grinned at him and shook my head while I reloaded. "Not tonight, Will. We've burned enough of Todd's powder."

"Aw, come on, Bud. Please."

I could see that Todd and Alf were as eager as Will, though they were too polite to press it. I stuck the pistol in my belt, all set to refuse, and then I caught sight of Stone Braden. He was watching me with narrowed eyes, a little possum smile on his face like he'd just confirmed something he'd known all along. A devil rose up in me, the way it had done when I'd killed the hawk with Johnnie watching.

"Let the deputy show you," I said. "You've told me how good he is with a gun."

Everybody's eyes went to Braden. He looked uncertain, but he wasn't about to let me back him down. He walked over to us, unlimbering his old revolver while Alf set up the cans that weren't too badly battered to use. Braden picked one on a waist-high limb, took aim with his arm out stiff. His ball knocked it off the limb, and he kicked it along the ground with two more shots. Then he lowered the hammer and looked at me.

"Your turn," he said.

I nodded. Will had started for the targets, but a word from Sheriff Stanton stopped him. He turned back toward me, looking from me to Braden as if he'd just realized we weren't close friends.

"Here, Will."

I brushed him back and out of the way with my left hand, pivoting toward the oak while my right snatched the Colt clear. The gun settled onto a tomato can like a bird dog going to point. My bullet grazed it, knocked it skittering sideways. The second shot caught it in the air, and the third sent it spinning out of sight in the brush.

"Wow!" Will said, goggle-eyed. "I never knew you were near so fast, Bud!"

"That's shooting!" Alf slapped his palms together. "You're a natural shooter, Bud. Reminds me of your pa, back in the old days."

"Aw, you could do it yourself, Alf," Todd joked. "If you used your Sharps, that is."

Sheriff Stanton frowned a little. "Being fast ain't everything, Will," he said. "There's lots of men in the cemetery today that thought being fast with a handgun made them something special."

Braden grinned at me like he figured that had hit me hard. It hadn't. The sheriff wasn't saying a word I didn't agree with. What puzzled me was Braden. I was pretty sure he'd taken his time on purpose, and that he was a lot quicker on the trigger than he'd let on. I remembered him in the back meadow that morning, watching me and Johnnie with his hand on his hip.

Probably the sheriff meant to go on to talk about using a pistol responsibly and staying out of trouble. Before he could finish, though, Alf Cryer spoke up.

"You're dead right about that, Amos," he said. "Drawing that hogleg ain't nothing if a man don't have the guts to use it. Time and again I seen it in the war—some feller who'd act every inch the soldier, then show the white feather when it come to fighting."

"That wasn't exactly what—"

"Like Bud here. He don't look like a killer, any more than his pa, but we know how he behaves when the chips are down, yes, sir."

I'd turned away when I saw how the talk was going

to go. Right then I didn't want to hear what a hero I was. That was the only reason I happened to be looking at Braden, and the expression on his face stopped me cold. The way he acted, you'd have thought Alf was talking straight to him. His face went pale, and he balled his fists like he wanted to fight. Then his eyes met mine, and he took a jerky step toward me.

"Tilden—"

Then Sheriff Stanton was on his feet, faster than I would've thought he could move. Without making it obvious, he put himself squarely between Braden and me.

"I'd guess that stew's about ready," he said mildly. He put an arm around Braden's shoulders. "Let's go see. I'm so hungry I could near eat one of them horses."

Braden stiffened against the arm, then relaxed and let himself be led off toward the fire. Will and the others followed. Except for the sheriff, none of them seemed to have noticed anything. They hadn't seen Braden's face. I had.

Maybe Alf didn't think I looked like a killer, but just for that second, Stone Braden did.

After supper I was ready to unroll my blankets and call it a day. I was almighty tired and still hurting, but mostly I wanted a chance to think. Between Ann's sudden change of heart, the things Alf had said about Pa, my experience with Johnnie and the hawk, and Braden's reaction to whatever had set him off, I'd had a pretty eventful day. But Will and Todd got started singing, and nothing would do but for the rest of us to join in. Braden didn't look any more eager than I was, but he pushed himself up from his seat against the old oak and came over to the fire.

"Got your harmonica, Stone?" Will called.

Braden fished a battered old mouth organ from his shirt pocket, took a couple of practice bleats, then began to play "The Dying Cowboy." It wasn't a very cheerful song, but it pretty well matched my feelings, so I sang along with the rest. We went from one tune to another for half an hour, probably scaring off every coyote in the county, and then the sheriff cleared his throat for attention.

"Probably we'd best mount a guard over the horses. I don't think we'll have trouble tonight, but it won't hurt to be careful. Alf, you want to start out?"

"Sure enough, Amos. Just like the old days."

Sheriff Stanton smiled. "I hope not," he said. He looked at each one of us, saving me and Braden for last. "Anybody mind if we finish with a hymn before we turn in?"

That was just like the sheriff. Nobody minded, of course, so he led us in "Abide with Me." It was a new song then. I didn't know the words past the first verse. Humming along and listening, I figured Amos Stanton had picked that one because the last stanza made a good prayer for the night:

Hold Thou Thy cross before my closing eyes;
Shine through the gloom and point me to the skies;
Heav'n's morning breaks, and all vain shadows flee:
In life, in death, O Lord, abide with me.

The crisp stroke of an ax brought me up, tangled in my blankets, scrabbling for my carbine. If I couldn't find it, the next blow of the ax would kill Davy. I felt a fingernail tear, but then the Winchester was in my hands, barely in time, because Trey Bonner was raising the ax, only he had Braden's face, and it wasn't Davy the blade was poised over, it was me—

Then I woke up. I was on my knees in the dry grass

of the Wells, the Winchester clutched in my hands. The sky had the clear, cold gray of a winter morning before sunup. Todd Milner was a shapeless bundle of blankets a couple of yards away, and Alf Cryer snored steadily over to my right. I didn't see Braden or the sheriff, but Will—

"Will! Stop that!"

Will turned from the pile of firewood to stare at me like I'd suddenly grown horns and a tail. The way he saw it, he was just being helpful, and he looked surprised and hurt. I got to my feet, feeling foolish, but before I could say anything Stone Braden came running from down by the creek.

"Don't yell at him." Braden planted himself in front of me. "He's just doing what I told him—cutting firewood so's we can cook breakfast."

Right then I wasn't in a mood for Braden. I shoved him away, none too gently.

"Suppose you tend to your own business, Deputy. You don't seem to be very good at that."

"Listen, Tilden, I've had about all—"

"That's enough."

Amos Stanton's voice wasn't loud, but it carried weight. Braden and I froze where we stood. The sheriff stepped between us. He was starting to make a habit of that, I thought.

"Stone, go on along now. Are you all right, Bud?"

I nodded, shamefaced. "Sorry. I was asleep. When I heard Will chopping . . ."

Will's gaze went from me to the ax in his hand, and his eyes widened in understanding. "Gosh, Bud, I'm sorry! I never thought—"

"It's all right," I said. "You didn't know."

The sheriff looked around, then chuckled. Todd and Alf were both out of their blanket rolls, goggling at us like we were the sideshow at a circus.

"Well, as long as we're all awake, we may as well get on the trail. If we're going to find the Willis boys, likely we'll do it today."

Grumbling and shaking their heads, the others gathered their gear. I pulled my boots on and followed Sheriff Stanton.

"Sheriff?" I asked when we were out of earshot. "You figure we'll find anything?"

He smiled at me. "Not really. Chances are, that wasn't even them in Waco. But I know the Willises. If they're in the neighborhood, I'm pretty sure where they'll go." He paused, and his face turned serious. "Bud, you ought to give Stone some room. He's a better man than you take him for."

I cinched my hat down. "Must be true," I said. "All the Stantons keep telling me so."

We were on the trail before sunrise, and this time I could tell where we were headed. The sheriff was leading us right toward my favorite hunting ground, the high meadow where I'd hid out after Davy was killed. We took it slow, keeping to the trees and brush even though there was a pretty good road not far to the south. About an hour before noon we came in sight of the narrow, rocky canyon that led up to the meadow.

"We'll let the horses breathe," the sheriff decided. "You all dismount and wait. I'm going to ride ahead a little and scout the road."

"Papa, let me come, too," Will said.

"Not now, son." Sheriff Stanton jerked his head at me and Braden. "Bud, Stone, come with me a minute."

He led us a few yards from the others, to a gap where we could see the road. "Listen," he said, as if he was showing us something down there. "I know you two young roosters are anxious to get your spurs into each other, but it's got to stop right now. Until we get back to town you're lawmen, nothing else. Understand?"

"Yes, sir," I said. Braden nodded.

"All right. Keep an eye on Will, should anything happen—not that I expect it."

He rode slowly down through the trees. Without saying anything I slid out of the saddle and threw my reins to Braden. Without saying anything he took them, so I got my rifle and climbed onto a boulder where I could see. Everything was as peaceful as a church. Except for a lone buzzard circling lazily across the high ridges, there wasn't a living thing in sight.

Presently the sheriff emerged onto the rutted road that would take a person to Waco if he rode far enough east. At that distance he looked like a little tin soldier posed stiffly on his horse. He dismounted, going to one knee to look at something in the road. As he knelt there I saw his body give a sudden sideways jerk. At first I thought he'd slipped, but then he spun halfway around and fell on his side in the road. I could have counted three before I heard the crack of the rifle echoing down from somewhere in that rocky canyon.

Chapter 10

I LEAPT OFF THE BOULDER, fell, and came up running for my horse. The others didn't know what had happened, and I wasn't taking time to explain.

"What the hell?" Cryer was yelling.

Todd stepped in front of me, and I swung up a hand to knock him aside. "Was that a shot?" he wanted to know.

Braden, at least, had the sense not to say anything. I vaulted into my saddle and snatched the reins from his hands. His face told me he already knew all he needed to.

"Look after Will." I was already kicking Reno to a gallop. As I tore out of the clearing I could hear Will's voice behind me.

"Wait! It's Papa, ain't it? Bud, wait up!"

I didn't answer and I didn't wait. Branches whipped across my face as I drove Reno through the brush. Just short of the road I piled off and let the horse go. I'd barely gotten clear when another bullet came singing down the canyon. I threw myself flat in a mess of brush and cactus, then started worming my way toward the road. I'd lost my rifle somewhere along the way, and the Colt, still in my saddlebag, might as well never have left the factory. A gun wasn't what I needed right then, anyway; I had to get to the sheriff.

Behind me another horse was coming fast. Will. He'd gotten away from Braden somehow, and he was making a dandy target of himself. He was almost to the gap in the trees where I'd drawn fire. I yelled, but the boy was hell-bent on reaching his pa. I got up and ran.

Bullets cut the brush around me. The muscles of my back tightened, waiting for one to hit, but I made the clearing just as Will got there. Driving hard, I threw myself against his pony's shoulder. The horse shied sideways, off balance, then came down in a screaming tangle at the foot of an oak. Dragging Will clear, I caught a flailing hoof on my forearm and another on the thigh. Finally the pony managed to find its feet and move away. Will was shaking his head dazedly, and I couldn't move my left arm or leg. Then the hidden rifleman started finding the range on our tree.

I was wrong; I could move, though it hurt like the mischief. Will's little varmint rifle was on the ground a couple of yards away. I started for it, then changed my mind and grabbed Will instead, dragging him to shelter behind the gnarled trunk of the oak. Just then Braden came in like a cavalry charge. In a second he was off his horse and standing in the open, firing his heavy pistol up the canyon.

He didn't have a chance of hitting anything, but he did distract the bushwhacker—though not for long. I dragged him down just as the rifleman pumped three rounds through the space where he'd been standing.

Maybe I saved his life, but neither of us was in a mood for thanks.

"Damn you! I told you to watch Will!"

"He got away! Let go of me!"

"Listen! Get that rifle and give me some cover. And keep Will here!"

"Where do you think—"

I didn't wait. Limping, but gradually working up to full stride, I made for the road again. My movement drew a bullet, so I dived behind a pile of rocks to get my breath. Then Will's .32-20 barked spitefully. Another rifle—Todd's Winchester, from the sound—spoke from above and behind us. I couldn't guess where Alf was, and right then I didn't care. It was time for me to go.

Braden might have read my mind, because he opened up again, shooting fast and accurately. In action, he was a different man from the one who'd fired so deliberately in practice, but I didn't have time to wonder about that. I rolled onto the road, came up in a crouch, and ran to where Sheriff Stanton lay.

The sheriff's eyes were open, but he didn't seem to see me. I bent over him, making myself as small as possible, praying that Todd and Braden could keep the rifleman busy.

"Sheriff! Amos! Can you move if I help you?"

He rolled his head back. "Hold Thou Thy cross before my closing eyes," he chanted tonelessly.

"Sheriff!"

A bullet kicked dirt a foot from his head. I couldn't wait any longer. I grabbed him under the armpits and dragged him toward the rockpile. He screamed once—a scream like Davy's—and then he was quiet. I was afraid he'd died, but when I bent over him in the shelter of the rocks he was still whispering, "In life, in death, O Lord." He drew in a breath and stopped.

As near as I could tell, a bullet had raked downward across his back, skimming two or three ribs and plowing a furrow that ended at his spine. There was a lot of blood, but none of it was fresh.

"Sheriff!"

"Abide—" He gave a shudder that lifted his upper body off the ground. "Bud. That you?"

"It's me. I've got you. You're not going to die."

He turned his eyes my way, and this time they were clear. "Willis." His voice got stronger. "Has he shot the horses?"

"No."

"It's Ed, then. Sol would've shot the horses."

The firing was still going on, shots coming from the canyon and Braden and Todd answering. A bullet whined off the rocks above us. I was beginning to wish for my carbine.

"Maybe it's both of them," I said.

"We'd be dead in the road." The sheriff closed his eyes again. "What's lying on my legs? Awful heavy."

I started to answer, decided he was better left alone. Stripping off my coat, I laid it over him, then crawfished my way to the edge of the rocks. The rifleman up the canyon came pretty near to putting a bullet through my head. Braden answered him at once. Then a big rock near the head of the canyon shattered like glass, throwing splinters every which way. An instant later I heard a dull boom far to my left. Alf Cryer had finally worked into position to use his Sharps.

That took some of the starch out of the bushwhacker. Alf was out of the gunman's effective range and high enough on the hillside so he could shoot straight into the canyon. One more bullet came my way, but it was the last. The Sharps boomed four or five more times without being answered. I took a chance and poked my head up.

"Braden?" I called. "You see him?"

"No. I'd be shooting."

"Bud!" That was Will. His voice said he'd been crying. "Bud, is my pa all right?"

"He's fine, Will. You stay right there till we're sure Willis is gone."

He didn't, of course. In less than a minute he was scrambling across to me. Braden followed, cursing. We huddled behind the rocks while Will made sure his pa was really alive.

"Milner's by the big tree where we started," Braden told me. He was watching the high ground, his hands tight on Will's Winchester. "Cryer worked back to get a clear shot. Took him long enough."

"Maybe, but he saved our skins when he got there. Do you have shells for that rifle?"

"Plenty. Will had his coat pockets full."

"All right. Me and Will are going to move the sheriff back where it's safer. You give us cover."

Braden started to balk at my giving the orders. Then he closed his lips into a tight line and nodded. "Go when you're ready."

With Braden covering us, we got Amos Stanton to the tree, picked up Todd, then fell back to the clearing where we'd first stopped to rest. We were sheltered there, but we still had a clear view of the mouth of the canyon. Braden joined us almost at once, and I went to round up the horses. Will's had pulled up lame from his fall, but the others were all right. Nobody shot at me.

When I got back Braden was working a bandage around the sheriff's back while Will watched anxiously.

"All that moving started him bleeding again," Braden said briefly. "We got to do something."

"What about Willis?"

Braden frowned. "He's long gone. He probably lit out as soon as Alf started shooting."

"Not unless he's walking. I've hunted that canyon and the meadow above it." I got the Colt from my saddlebag and stuck it through my belt. My carbine was still down the hill somewhere, so I drew the sheriff's rifle from its boot. "It's like a bowl, with the sides too steep and rocky to get a horse down. He's got to come out the way he went in."

Almost without being noticed, Alf Cryer had drifted in from the woods and taken station behind a boulder, his Sharps trained on the canyon mouth. "Nobody's coming out this way," he said, slapping the stock of his rifle. "Not while it's light enough to see."

"The hell with Willis," Will put in suddenly. His whole body was trembling, and Todd Milner went and put an arm around him. "We got to get Pa in. He has to have a doctor."

"No!"

I hadn't even realized the sheriff was conscious, but his voice was almost as strong as ever. He caught at Braden's wrist.

"Deputy, you're in charge. That's Ed Willis up there. See you get him."

"Yes, sir," Braden said. He shot me a look with none of his little smile in it. He looked ten years older. "We'll get him."

The sheriff nodded, but that seemed to use up all his strength. He leaned back again and closed his eyes, his hands rubbing his thighs like they were cold.

"Papa!" Will was almost sobbing. "What about Pa? He's bleeding bad!"

"Listen, Will," I said. "You've got to ride to town. Take your pa's horse. Bring back the doctor and a wagon." Then I remembered Braden was in charge. "All right, Deputy?"

"I can make it quicker on the gray," Alf said.

Braden looked angry, then thoughtful. "No," he said slowly. "Will's the lightest." He nodded to the boy. "Go, Will. Ride hard."

Will didn't argue. He was aboard the sheriff's road horse in one jump. In another second he'd reined the animal around and was pounding back the way we'd come.

"It wasn't my place to do that," I told Braden, quietly enough so the others didn't hear. "But I figured it'll be better if Will's not here."

"You think . . ." Whatever Braden was going to ask, he glanced at the sheriff and changed his mind. "You were right," he admitted. "Just don't forget I'm calling the shots."

It grated on me a little, but I remembered my promise to the sheriff. "Dollar a day and beans either way," I said.

"All right. We'll have to camp here. Todd, if you'll sit with Sheriff Stanton, I'll take the horses back in the trees. Alf, you stay put. Tilden . . ." He looked at me like he expected an argument. "It'll be dark soon. I wish you'd work down close to the road and watch that canyon so Willis doesn't slip out."

"Thank I can handle it?"

"I know you can," he said grimly. "I know you can shoot a man, if it comes to that."

Carrying the sheriff's rifle and a canteen, I stuffed a couple of breakfast biscuits into one coat pocket and a box of shells into the other, then took a stand under the oak where Will and I had been pinned down. By now the sun was behind the hills. I strained my eyes watching the canyon, trying to pick out any movement among the shifting shadows. I was sure Willis was still there. He might have followed the canyon up to where the land flattened out, but that was as far as he could get. I'd hunted every inch of the woods around that meadow, and I knew there was no other trail down. Unless he was ready to try walking out, he could come back down the canyon or wait for us to come up after him.

Just before full dark Alf Cryer slipped down as quiet as an Indian and crouched beside me.

"How's the sheriff?" I asked him.

"Tolerable." His voice wouldn't have carried ten feet. "We got the bleeding stopped."

"Can he move his legs?"

"Not yet." Alf looked away. "Supper's done. You want to come back to camp?"

"I'll stay. We've got him bottled up. I'm not going to uncork the bottle now."

"You can't see him! Suppose he sneaks down here and cuts your throat?"

I'd thought a little about that, too. "As soon as it's darker, I'm going up into the mouth of the canyon," I said. "Unless Willis is part bat, he can't climb down the sides in the dark. If he comes out, horseback or afoot, he'll have to come past me. I'll see him."

"You'll get hungry. Sleepy, too."

"I'll manage."

Alf took a plug of tobacco from his shirt pocket and gnawed at it thoughtfully. "You're old Henry's kid all right. Get an idea in your head, and it's awful hard to get out." He slipped the barrel of his Sharps past the tree and aimed it up the canyon. "Moonrise in about two hours. Keep to the east side, so we'll know where you'll be if anything happens. Want any help?"

"Not up there. I need to know who I'm shooting at. Just watch the horses tonight, in case he gets by me."

Alf snorted. "Boy, don't tell your grandmother how to suck eggs. Nobody ever stole a horse from Old Bedford's men."

"That was a long time ago."

"I haven't forgot," he said. "No more has your pa, I expect." Squinting over the sights of the Sharps, he waved a hand at me. "You be careful, Bud. Go now, and I'll cover you."

I went.

The night was as long as I'd ever seen. Even wrapped in my coat and hunkered down out of the wind, I was cold enough to shiver. I tried to be quiet about it, because I expected Willis to come down after me. His chances were a lot better than they'd be in the morning, so I tensed at every little sound. Even so, I dozed once or twice, to snap awake from a dream of a man behind me—a man with Braden's face. When the moon set without Willis turning up, I began to wonder if Alf or Braden had hit him during all the shooting.

Who came instead was Braden, catfooting it up the canyon during the coldest and quietest part of the night. When he got even with my hiding place I whistled like a bobwhite. It almost gave him a runaway, but then he ducked into the shadows. He had his rifle and canteen, and a pair of saddlebags slung over his shoulder.

"The others are gone," he told me. "Doc Wisenhunt came with a wagon. I sent Alf and Todd to help with Sheriff Stanton." I thought I could see his little smile. "Now it's just you and me."

"Is the sheriff all right?"

"Doc says he'll probably live."

"Will he walk?"

"I asked that, too." Braden shrugged. "Doc said he wasn't God, so he didn't know. The bullet bounced off his backbone. Could be that the nerves are just bruised—or it could be that a piece of bone cut his spinal cord." He paused a second, then added, "Dragging him around all over the country probably didn't help him much."

"Leaving him in the road to get shot again wouldn't have helped him much either."

Braden didn't answer.

"Listen," I said. "You know what really happened."

"Sure. You went charging through all those bullets and dragged the sheriff out. You were a real hero."

I'd got so I didn't care if I ever heard that word again. "Is that how you're going to tell it?"

He gave me that smile. "No occasion for me to tell anything," he said. "Everybody knows you're a hero."

I remembered what saloon talk had made of Davy's killing and of my fight with Mayfield. Maybe Braden had helped twist the truth then, too. I started an answer, then took a minute to relax and cool down. Willis was still up the canyon someplace, might still decide to come down. We couldn't afford to get too wrapped up in arguing.

Finally I said, "Braden, you've had something against me from the start. I thought it was Annette—"

"A gentleman," he interrupted coldly, "doesn't discuss a lady—"

"That lets us out, then. Anyway, it started before that—almost the first time you saw me."

"That's right," Braden said. "The very first time." He shifted position to squint at the sky. "It'll keep. We've got a job to do. Maybe you can be a hero again."

"Maybe I can get shot in the back."

He laughed softly. "Not by me. Not in the back. Gentlemen—"

"I know," I told him. "Gentlemen don't shoot gentlemen in the back."

Such as it was, our plan was simple. Braden would work along one wall of the canyon. I'd take the other. If Willis tried to ride out, he'd have to go between us. If we didn't come across him before we reached the top, we'd wait for daybreak and decide what to do next. We ate cold biscuits and bacon from Braden's saddlebags. Then he dashed across to the west side while I covered him, and we started to climb.

Ahead of us, dark walls rose against a sky just going gray. Angular rocks were tumbled along either side, a dandy place to break a leg floundering around in the dark. If we waited until full light, though, Willis could see to shoot. I agreed with Braden's thinking, but I didn't like it any. The whole way up I had my rifle cocked and ready, expecting to find Willis behind every bush.

At the upper reach of the canyon the trail ran through a narrow cut in the brush. I hadn't seen anything of Braden from the first, but I hoped he was covering my flank while I covered his. Gentlemen, I decided, should have had sense enough to plan a signal. Finally I tried the bobwhite call again, realizing too late that I'd given my location to two men who might want to shoot me. After about ten seconds one of them whistled back from the far side of the trail. Willis wouldn't have whistled. I snaked my way to a dead tree just where the canyon started to open out. Pushing the rifle out in front of me, I waited for the sun to top the rim.

In the first sunlight the meadow was quiet and empty. A morning breeze rustled the tall brown grass. The sides of the meadow sloped up gradually into brush and trees, still black and indistinct. Willis had to be someplace among them.

I heard something moving behind me and swiveled around, keeping the rifle ready.

"Don't shoot," Braden whispered. He had dropped back downhill to cross the trail and find me. "Can you see him?"

"Nope. He's in the brush. If he knows we're here, he'll wait till we show ourselves. If not, he should be moving soon."

Braden frowned. I could see there were some problems to being in charge. The morning was still cold, but sweat stood out on his forehead. He licked his lips and scanned the meadow.

"I'm going in," he said at last. He swallowed hard. "You stay here and see he doesn't get down the trail. I'll drive him out to you."

"Sounds like a good way for you to get shot."

He grinned—a real grin, not his tight smile. "In the back?"

"Wherever. What do you think you are, a hero?"

"Maybe." He looked hard at me, and the moment when we'd understood each other was gone. "Listen, I want him alive—not your usual way. I'm telling you."

"I've known Amos Stanton since I was six."

"That doesn't matter."

"Maybe not to you."

"That's how the sheriff wants it. I'm telling you."

"You've told me," I said. "Better get along, hero."

I took my post by the dead tree, with a good view of the meadow and the upper part of the trail. Braden drew a deep breath, then plunged across the open cut and into the thicket on the far side. I didn't envy him his job. Wounded or not, Willis was apt to be as dangerous as a cornered grizzly. At least, I thought, he wouldn't know there were only two of us. He'd figure we were coming with a real army.

For what seemed like hours, nothing much happened. Braden flushed a flock of crows that took off with a cawing and clatter like Judgment Day. A woodpecker went to work somewhere, scaring me out of a year's growth. The sun began to warm my back so that I was sweating, but I didn't dare to take my coat off. Looking from below, I occasionally caught a patch of movement or a glint of sunlight on the deputy's badge, but that was all. Then a rangy brown horse came walking out of the trees not far ahead of where I'd last seen Braden. The brown lifted its head to the morning breeze and started straight for me.

For a dozen long seconds I was too surprised to think. The horse was saddled and bridled. He started out walking, then broke into a trot. By the time I realized riderless horses didn't behave that way, he was making full stride for the canyon trail.

Braden ran out of the trees, waving and yelling. I didn't look his way. I'd picked up the brown neck in my rifle sights, leading the horse like he was a buck crossing the meadow. The Winchester fired, and a patch of red blossomed just behind his shoulder. He made one more stumbling step, then rolled over hard on his neck and shoulder.

I heard Braden yell again, but I already had another shell in the chamber. A man bobbed up from behind the horse's body where he'd been clinging like an Indian. His movements were stiff and jerky, but he had a rifle in his hands. I didn't know or care if he meant to use it. I shot him, and he threw up his hands and fell across the horse.

The deputy went running toward two bodies. I didn't hurry. Both shots had gone right where I'd aimed them. I knew, the way I could tell sometimes on a hunt. Braden was beside Willis, his fists balled, when I got close enough to see the blood.

"Sorry," I said. "He didn't want to go in alive."

Braden didn't say a word, just came at me like a rock from a slingshot. His shoulder smashed into my middle and took me clean off my feet. I lost the rifle and went down with him on top, pounding away at my head with both fists. I got my forearms up to block most of the blows, then rolled like a sunfishing bronc to throw him off.

He lit on his knees and elbows and came scrambling back fierce as a badger. I caught him with a solid lick to the side of the head as he was coming in. It slowed him down, but my hand felt like I'd punched an anvil. I hit him again, and then he was back on top, digging short punches into my ribs—no way to treat a man who'd been shot there not so long before. Somehow I managed to throw him off again. This time I went right after him, hooking to his jaw and nose, feeling his lips split and seeing his left eye start to swell closed.

All I could think of was smashing that smile of his. I never even noticed he was hitting me back until I realized I was lying on my face with my mouth full of dirt. Something limp and heavy lay halfway across me. I jabbed at it with an elbow and got a feeble kick in return. I was trying to decide to get up and finish things when Alf Cryer's voice broke through the clouds that must have come up while we were fighting.

"What the hell?" Braden's weight went away, and Alf seemed to get closer. "Look at yourselves! Here, quit it! What in tarnation happened here?"

I'd been wondering that myself, but I settled for spitting out a mouthful of blood and dry grass. My shirt looked like I'd been butchering hogs. From what I could see of Braden, he wasn't any better off.

"I saw the others down to the road with the sheriff,

then came back," Alf was saying. "Good thing, too. Why were you two trying to beat each other to death?"

Braden ignored him. Raising his head, the deputy turned his one good eye on me.

"You didn't have to do that," he muttered thickly.

"What?"

"Willis. Could—taken him alive."

"Like hell. He'd have shot one of us—maybe both."

Braden wiped his face with a tattered sleeve. "You meant to kill him all along," he said. "Never meant to get him alive. Killer, that's what you are. You're a killer, right down to the bone."

Chapter 11

WE HADN'T MUCH MORE THAN GOTTEN STARTED back to town when we met Todd Milner leading out an army to help us. Every able-bodied man in town plus a few that weren't must have turned out when the doc brought Sheriff Stanton in. Judge Poe, who hadn't sat a horse in years, was driving his buggy. Tom Perry sat beside him, saying over and over, "I knew I should've gone with them. This would never have happened to Amos if I'd been along."

Pa was in the group, looking sad and sorrowful when he saw the Colt in my belt, and Avery Thomas, and a lot more I recognized, right down to Crabtree and some of his cronies from the Palace. Every man had a rifle, and the judge's buggy held enough ammunition to refight the Alamo.

I was mighty happy to see them because I was on foot. Ed Willis, wrapped in a poncho, was roped across my saddle. Reno didn't like that arrangement much more than I did, but it had been the deputy's orders.

"You killed him," Braden had said. "You carry him."

There was some justice in that; besides, he was still in charge, and I hadn't given him the satisfaction of arguing about it.

When the new posse met us, pulling out of its gallop in a tangle of shouting men and nervous horses, Judge Poe looked first at the body.

"Who's shot?" he demanded. "Deputy, what happened?"

"It's Willis," Braden said thickly. "One of them. Ed, the sheriff said."

"Willis!" Judge Poe stood up in the buggy and shouted to the rest. "Hear that, boys? They got Ed Willis!" He caught his first clear sight of Braden's face, then of mine. "He must have put up quite a fight. You two look like you've been sorting wildcats."

"Hell, that weren't Willis," Alf Cryer put in. "They done that to each other. Good thing I came back to stop them, or they might've"—I caught his eye and he broke off, then finished lamely—"might've hurt one another."

Judge Poe looked puzzled. "Well—" he began, but Crabtree and some of his friends interrupted.

"There he is!" Crabtree had cut the ropes and yanked back the poncho we had over Willis. "Don't seem so tough now, does he?"

I didn't look. I'd seen enough of Ed Willis. He'd been a scrawny, wiry sort of man, with a hard face and a scraggly beard. His clothes were stiff with dirt and blood, only part of it from my bullet. He'd also had a wound low in his belly, older and crusted over, with the bullet still inside. It must have given him plenty of misery. Probably it was the reason he hadn't tried to break out the night before.

"The sheriff-shooting son of a bitch!" Crabtree cried. He fired his rifle into the air, and so did a couple of other idiots. "Get a rope! Let's hang him up right here for a warning!"

"Now hold on!" Braden yelled. "It's my job to bring him in."

I pushed at the men and horses crowding me, but without much luck. It was the judge who restored order.

"Wait, now! Just wait! Put away your guns!" He was using his speechmaking voice. "Let these brave men tell us what happened!" He turned to Braden. "Which of you got him?"

Braden jerked his thumb at me. "Tilden," he growled. "He deserves every bit of credit for the shooting."

Most of the judge's posse heard that, and they passed the word to the rest. I didn't know how they'd take it. Some of them set up a cheer. Alf and Todd joined in, but Pa didn't. Then Crabtree and his gang started yelling.

"That's Bud! That's our man, Judge. He's the one!"

I didn't know what they were talking about, and I wasn't a bit sure I wanted to be their man. Still, I'd had about enough of Braden's hazing because I'd shot a man who'd crippled Sheriff Stanton. It felt good to have somebody side with me, even the likes of Crabtree. I felt even better when Todd and some of the other solid men took it up.

Judge Poe raised his hand for quiet. "We might've known Bud would be the hero," he said, combing his beard. "You all have said it better than I could. He's the man for the job." He motioned to me. "Bud, come over here."

I went, not knowing what to expect. The judge beamed down at me.

"Bud, we're beholden to you again," he said. "I know the whole county's grateful, and I'm sure your pa is mighty proud." He raised his voice. "Folks, I'm going to announce something right here. You all know Amos is out of action, at least temporarily. So until his recovery or election time, I'm appointing Bud Tilden here to be acting sheriff!"

It caught me cold; I couldn't think what to say. Then they all started clapping and cheering—all but Braden. He looked too whipped and miserable to live. I should've been happy to see his smile wiped off, but—except for the first few seconds—I wasn't. I had to admit he'd been trying his best, and this seemed like a poor reward. Before I could do anything he shot me a long, bitter look, then spurred his little chestnut away from the crowd and off toward town.

Then men were pounding me on my sore back, congratulating me and offering to take Willis off my hands. I mumbled my thanks to the judge. Finally, I saw they expected me to give some orders. Being a farmer hadn't given me much practice, but I made a try.

"Mr. Perry, I'd appreciate it if you'd take charge of the body and get it into town—without hanging." That made them laugh. "I need to clean up a little. Then I'll get started at my duties."

After a little more talk I got away. My first thought was to head for my place, but Pa overtook me on the road. I expected him to bring up the Colt, or my shooting Willis. He didn't.

"You might as well come home with me, Bud," he said instead. "You'll have to come into town anyway, and you'll want Doc Wisenhunt to look at that eye." I waited for his anger, but it didn't come. "It's mighty good to have you back safe, son," was all he said.

Ma had quite a bit more to say, especially after she heard about my fight with Braden.

"I declare, I don't know what's got into you. Fighting with that nice deputy. The very idea!"

By that time I'd had a long soak in a tub of hot water and some clean clothes. Shaving hadn't been easy, because it hurt just to look at my face in a mirror, but I'd managed. All that and a cup of Ma's coffee made me feel like I might last out the rest of the day.

"The fight was his idea, Ma," I told her. "He didn't give me a whole lot of choice about it."

"The very idea!" she repeated. "That cut over your eye needs stitches."

"No."

"It'll leave a scar."

"Then I'll just have to have one." I put down the cup and stood up. "I promised I'd get over to the sheriff's office as soon as I could."

To see what her nice deputy had been up to, I added silently. Braden's expression before he rode off worried me.

"Be careful, Bud," Pa said. Looking at him, I tried to fit him to a uniform and a gun, but it just didn't seem right.

"Mr. Cryer told me you rode with him in the old days," I said. I heard Ma's quick intake of breath. "Figured he was just spinning tales."

"No," Pa said slowly. He looked at the Colt at my waist and frowned. "Alf's a good man. We ought to talk about that sometime."

He hadn't asked me any questions. I figured I owed him the same courtesy.

"All right. See you later."

"Come back for supper," Ma called, like I was still nine years old. "And don't you be fighting again!"

I'd planned to go straight to the sheriff's office, but a sudden impulse took me to the Stanton house instead. I hadn't heard any word on Sheriff Stanton, and I was anxious about him. Besides, I wanted to see Annette.

Will met me at the door. "Hi, Bud," he said. "They're all in the kitchen. Come in."

Inside, he looked over my cuts and bruises like I was a horse he was thinking of buying, but he didn't mention them.

"How's your pa?" I asked. I handed him Amos's rifle that I'd been using.

"All right, I guess. Brother Winslow's with him."

"That bad, is he?"

"No, they're just talking." Will looked at my face again, then stepped closer to me. "I don't care what anybody says," he said in a low, tight voice. "I'm glad you killed Willis—except I wanted to do it myself." He turned away quickly, motioning toward a door. "They're in the bedroom. Go on in."

Amos Stanton was sitting up in bed with a couple of pillows behind him, like he had nothing more than a cold. He turned his head when I came in, but his lower body didn't move. Brother Winslow popped up from his chair and came to shake my hand. Both of them looked as if they were measuring my injuries against a standard they'd already seen.

"I didn't mean to break in on anything,' I said. "I just wanted to see how the sheriff was feeling."

"Tolerable well, Bud, thanks to you. Come on over here."

Close up, his face was deadly pale and he looked years older. His handshake, though, was as quick and firm as ever.

"Not sheriff any more, I understand." His pale eyes studied me, seeing past the bruises this time. "I hear you got the job after you brought down Willis."

"Just until you're on your—until you're better." I could've bitten my tongue off. "It was Judge Poe's doing. I hope I can handle the job."

Amos Stanton didn't smile. "It's not easy," he said. "A lawman can't let his personal feelings get in the way of duty."

"I don't know what you mean."

"Bud, you showed plenty of grit hauling me off that road. Saved my life, probably, and I'm grateful." He shook his head slowly. "Then you killed a man you might have brought in alive, and you fought with the deputy in charge."

"It took two to make that fight. I didn't start it."

He didn't show any sign of believing me. "You've gotten as quick with your temper as you are with a gun—but there's more to being sheriff than using a gun."

"I know that."

"Here," the preacher said quickly. "Have a chair, Bud."

I shook my head. "I've got to be going. Glad to see you're all right."

"Mighty good of you," Brother Winslow said. "I'll walk you out to the porch. I've been meaning to ask after your parents."

He came with me into the front room, closing the bedroom door behind him. I figured he had some more good advice to give me. By now I'd had about all I needed. "If you're going to say I shouldn't—" I began, but then Annette came from the back with an armload of towels. She stopped when she saw us, and her face went red as blood.

"Hello, Ann," I said.

She bit her lip. She was mad, but I didn't know if it was aimed at me or not. "Bud, you wait right here," she said. "I have to take these to the kitchen. I want to talk to you."

She pushed through the kitchen door without looking back. We went on outside to stand on the porch. Brother Winslow looked at the sky and combed his beard.

"Well, we can have our talk later on," he allowed. "I really wasn't going to give you a sermon, but I'm sure you'd rather spend the time with Annette."

I thought of telling him that Ann and I would be coming to see him before long, but it didn't seem like the right time to bring it up. Instead, I said, "Thanks, Preacher. I'm sorry if I got my back up."

"Take care of yourself, Bud." He started back inside, then turned and grinned at me. "For what it's worth, I'm on your side," he said, and he closed the door behind him.

I leaned back against the railing and closed my eyes. My knuckles were so swollen that it hurt to flex my fingers, but I gripped the wooden rail anyway, feeling the raw skin split open and start to bleed. When I'd first ridden in I'd felt pretty much like a hero, just like the judge had said. Since then it seemed that everybody I met had been acting as if I was the desperado and Willis and Braden were the victims. I was getting downright tired of it, too.

I heard the door close, and there was Ann. Wrapped in her green coat, she looked at me in a way I'd seen before—like I was somebody she didn't quite know. Her eyes today showed more green than brown. I put my arms out to her.

"Lord, Ann, I'm glad to see you. These last few days—"

She moved out of reach. "You've been fighting with Stone," she said.

"That's right." There was no point in denying it. My face would have convinced any jury.

"Why? Was it—because of me?"

Ann was plenty smart enough to figure that out for herself. Maybe she just wanted to hear me say it, but she probably didn't expect the answer that I gave her.

"Partly it was over you. Partly it was because of Willis. There's another part, too, one I don't know anything about. You'll have to ask Braden."

"I did. While—" She stopped and bit her lip. "While Mama and I were fixing him up in the kitchen," she finished slowly.

I remembered the towels she'd been carrying. "I see. I hope I didn't interrupt anything." Braden had used the same words when he'd come upon me and Johnnie.

"Bud! What do you think of me?"

"I think you spend a lot of time with Braden for somebody who's said she wants to marry me right away."

She turned away, going to stand beside the porch swing. I moved up behind her and put my hands on her shoulders.

"That was you, wasn't it, Ann? Remember that?"

"I remember." Her voice was almost a whisper. "But maybe—maybe we ought to wait."

"Why?"

She swung around to face me, almost against my chest, looking up into my eyes. "Bud, did you really have to kill that man? Stone says—"

"The hell with what Stone says!"

Ann cringed back like she'd been hit. I'd never spoken to her that way before, but I'd flat heard enough of Stone Braden.

"No, I didn't have to kill him," I told her. "I could've let him trot that horse right past me, so he could kill Mr. Cryer on the trail and ride off to cripple another sheriff or two. Would you have liked that better?"

She started to cry. "Bud, I don't want them to carry you home someday the way Papa is—or worse." She clenched her fists against her chest. "I don't want my children to have a—a killer for their father."

"I was just as much a killer that day in Hart's stable, after I'd shot Trey Bonner," I said. "You didn't seem to mind that so much. Maybe I should've taken what you were offering me then."

The slap had all her weight, and I guess all the anger and sorrow she was feeling, behind it. Smashing into the side of my bruised face, it hurt worse than anything Braden had hit me with. I caught my breath and grabbed the supports of the swing to keep from hitting back.

"Oh." Ann realized what she'd done. She reached out to touch my cheek, then pulled up short, putting both hands to her mouth instead. "I don't know who you are, Bud," she whispered. "You're a different person."

Her shoulders shaking, she spun away and ran into the house, slamming the door behind her. I put my hand up to the cut by my eye. My fingers came away bloody. "I haven't changed so much," I said aloud, but there was no one to hear.

I'd figured the sheriff's office would be a good place to be alone and think. It wasn't my day for being right. When I opened the door and stepped inside I found Stone Braden digging through a drawer of Amos Stanton's desk. When he saw me he slammed it closed and straightened quickly.

"Lose something?" I asked him.

"Just getting my gear together. The sheriff—Mr. Stanton—had been letting me bunk here."

"Why?"

He flushed. "Because I didn't have anyplace else to stay," he snapped. "That's what you've been telling me, isn't it? That I'm an outsider?"

"No, I mean why are you packing up?"

Braden's laugh wasn't a pretty sound. He yanked off his deputy's badge and threw it across the desk toward me.

"Did you think I was going to wait for you to run me out, Mister Sheriff? I know you'd have liked that, but I'll beat you to it."

I stared at him. I hadn't for a minute thought things through that far, but now I did. Judge Poe had appointed me sheriff. That meant Braden worked for me—or he had. All I needed to do was stand there another minute, and he'd be gone, buggy and all. It was a mighty tempting prospect.

"Well, why don't you say something? Tell me to get out of the county, maybe? Isn't that what sheriffs do with drifters and undesirables?"

The trouble was, I couldn't quite see myself doing it. Back on the trail, I would've gladly finished pounding Braden into mush. But I couldn't forget how he'd stood in the open to return Willis's fire, or the way he'd gone into the brush after the outlaw because he'd felt it was his job. None of that made me like him any better, but Amos Stanton had said something true: A lawman couldn't let his personal feelings interfere with his duty—and I was supposed to be a lawman now.

"Judge Poe and the county commissioners approved hiring you," I said. "It's not up to me to fire you."

It was his turn to stare at me. "Who's it up to, then?" He didn't trust me a nickel's worth.

"Besides, it'd be handy to have a deputy staying here, where folks can find him any time. Until I can arrange somebody to look after the farm, I'll have to be out—"

"Damn you, don't play with me!"

"Look, I can't stop you from quitting if you want to. But I didn't figure a gentleman like you to walk out on a job. If you want to stay on and try to make a go of it, I'm willing."

Braden blinked at me. Suddenly he relaxed, leaning heavily against the desk. "You really mean it, don't you?" Then he stiffened his back again. "Don't think it's going to make us friends, Tilden!"

If my face would have let me, I'd have grinned. Whatever had been stuck in his craw was still there, but for the first time I felt I'd bested him at the game we were playing.

"Just don't forget I'm calling the shots."

He must've remembered his words. His eyes said he had his doubts, but his mouth was fighting a smile.

"Dollar a day and beans either way," he said.

Chapter 12

I FOUND A BADGE—an extra Sheriff Stanton had kept, I suppose—in the top drawer of the desk and pinned it on my shirt. Braden went over the reports with me, told me we had no prisoners in the jail just then, and showed me the keys for the cells, the gun rack and ammunition drawers, and the two big oak file cabinets where the county tax records were stored.

"How about the desk?" I asked. "Doesn't it lock?"

His eyes shifted away, then came back to me. "Key's lost," he said. He scuffed at the floor with the toe of one boot. "Look, Til—Sheriff, all the monthly reports are up to date, and you can read the records for yourself. If you won't be needing me, I'm supposed—supposed to be somewhere."

Looking at him, I had a pretty good idea where he was headed. It didn't seem to matter much. I figured my temper had about finished things between me and Ann anyway.

"Sure. I'll see you first thing in the morning."

Braden might have given me that mean-mouthed smile, only I'd fixed his mouth so he wouldn't be smiling much for a while. It wasn't any great satisfaction to me. For every time I'd hit him, he'd landed at least once in return. That and the long night waiting to go after Willis had me hurting in every joint and tired enough to die. Right then I didn't care where he went, just so he let me stretch out and rest. He hadn't quite reached the door, though, when it swung open. A gust of cold air came in, followed by a huge, shaggy buffalo coat with a huge, shaggy man inside it.

"Stone Braden," I said, "meet Matthew MacNally."

Matthew was holding a long rifle in a fringed leather scabbard. He looked first at Braden's face, then at mine, last at the star on my shirt. Whatever he thought, none of it showed in his face. After a second he looked more closely at my deputy.

"Braden?" he said.

"That's right."

They exchanged cautious nods. Neither of them offered a hand. "You put me in mind of somebody," Matthew said slowly. He jerked his head in my direction. " 'Course, it might be him, seeing you both look like you've been tromped by the same bronc. I got business with the sheriff."

"I'm it," I told him. "Come in and get next to the stove."

It was only after he stepped inside that I saw Johnnie standing in his shadow. She wasn't as good as Matthew at hiding her feelings. Her eyes went round when she caught sight of me. She looked at Braden, and her lips tightened into a prim line. I wasn't sure why at first, but then I saw she was fit to burst from trying not to laugh.

"Hello, Johnnie," I said, a little bit nettled at her. "You've met Deputy Braden."

"Why, Deputy, I hardly recognized you," Johnnie said sweetly. "The last time we met you were dressed differently."

"John Catherine!" Matthew growled.

Braden cleared his throat. "I reckon the sheriff, here, was dressed differently, too." He looked at me. "I'll be going now. If it's all right with you. Sir."

I nodded. He brushed past Matthew and went off into the gathering dusk. Matthew hadn't moved, and it came to me he wasn't entirely comfortable in the sheriff's office.

"You're wearing Amos's badge," he said.

"My badge, for now. Until he gets better, at least."

Matthew snorted. "If," he said. Then he eyed me speculatively. "You might do. You'll need yourself a gun belt."

He was right, just as he'd been right about how long I'd live without packing a gun. Even so, I'd had all the advice I wanted for a while. "Did you find Luke?" I asked him.

He stared hard at Johnnie. She ignored him. She'd been looking at the cut over my eye.

"You're hurt. That needs stitches."

"I have a little money due me," Matthew said. "You know the kind I mean. I'll ask you to send for it proper-like."

"Money?" I asked.

He looked at me as though I was stupid, and maybe I was. "For the Willises. You'll be getting the other half." He put his rifle on the desk and came around closer to the stove. "You got Ed. I left Sol over at the icehouse. I'll need you to identify the body and claim the reward."

I thought about Ed Willis lying in the high meadow

with fresh bright blood across his chest and dark dried blood at his belt. "Then Ed was carrying your bullet," I said.

"Likely. Couldn't be sure, because my horse was down, but I figured I'd hit him." He shook his head. "I've known those old boys ten years or more; never thought we'd end up shooting at each other. Ran across them over by Gentry's Mill. They knew me right off, must've figured I was in their way." He grinned, and I felt a little surprise that his teeth weren't pointed like a bear's. "Which I was, after Sol shot my horse."

"I'll take care of the paperwork first thing tomorrow."

"Obliged. If I'm not around, leave the money with Johnnie." He strode to the far wall and lifted a gun belt off a wooden peg. "Who owns this?"

"Sheriff Stanton took it off some drifter, I expect. Why?"

Matthew drew the pistol from the holster, looked at it critically, then laid it on the desk. He held out belt and holster to me. "Try it on. Then try that fancy Colt in it."

The belt could've been a little tighter, but it would do. The holster was a different story. It clung to the silver Colt like molasses.

"Well, that'll keep you from losing your pistol, but you'll want some better leather soon's you can find it." He picked up his rifle and headed for the door. "Try to stay alive. I'd appreciate your seeing Johnnie home soon's she's done sewing you up."

Johnnie MacNally had taken off her coat and gloves. She had the stove lid open, and she was heating a needle in the licking flames.

"Now wait a minute," I told her.

"Where do you keep your whiskey?"

"I don't. Listen, I don't need any looking after."

She was rummaging through the desk the way Braden had done. Pretty soon she came upon a little flask tucked in among a pile of papers. An envelope addressed to Sheriff Stanton was right under the bottle, and I picked it up to see if it might be important.

"You sit over there." Johnnie had uncorked the flask and was dipping the needle in it. "Close your eyes."

I'd noticed before that Johnnie had a stubborn streak. This time, bucking her just didn't seem worth the trouble. Besides, the eye did need attention, and knowing Johnnie's brothers, I figured she'd had plenty of practice. She poured a generous slug of whiskey into the cut and wiped it away. I winced.

"Sorry," Johnny murmured. "In just a minute you won't feel it. Here, take a good mouthful. No, don't swallow!"

The whiskey seemed to take about half the skin out of my throat. I grinned up at Johnnie while she scolded me.

"Bud, you stop that! All right, take another one and *hold it* in your mouth."

I held the mouthful of whiskey until my teeth went numb. By then she was finished, without me ever feeling the needle. That would be a useful trick to remember if I was going to keep pounding my head against people's fists.

"There," Johnnie said, admiring her needlework. "You can spit that out."

I swallowed it. "Thank you," I said. I stood up, and the room took a slow turn around, only partly from the whiskey. "I'd be honored now to see you home."

Johnnie looked at me suspiciously. "I can get home by myself," she snapped.

"Your brother left you in my keeping," I reminded her. "I'd be honored to see you home."

"My brother . . ." she began. Then she stopped. "All right."

We put on our coats and blew out the lamp, and we were on our way. A half hour before I would've traded Reno for a rocking chair and thrown in my saddle. Now the ride out to MacNally's didn't seem like a bit of trouble. Either the whiskey or Johnnie had made quite a difference in the way I looked at things. Maybe it was just that Matthew and Johnnie seemed to accept what had happened without a whole lot of judging whether I'd been right or wrong.

Even though the MacNally place was just across the ridge from mine, their road led out of town another way, past the church. I turned up my collar as we passed the Stanton house. Johnnie noticed as surely as I did that Braden's buggy was standing outside. He'd had to walk to the livery to get it, then drive it back. That much trouble didn't make sense unless he'd planned to use it later, maybe for a drive with Annette.

Thinking about that didn't get me anywhere, so I turned back to what I was doing. Johnnie wasn't very talkative, and the brisk wind encouraged us to move along smartly and not waste words. About four miles out we topped a long rise and turned into a wooded lane to the right. I'd never come at their place from this direction, and it seemed different. The tall old house with its one round tower in front stood white and lonely in the moonlight. Proud oaks guarded its back and sides like sentries. Johnnie seemed different, too, quieter and less sure of herself than usual.

"Guess you can manage from here," I said. "Good night, Johnnie."

"No," she said quickly. She looked down at her

hands on the reins. "I mean, you must be starved. Come inside and get warm. Mark's probably got supper waiting."

In all that had happened, I'd forgotten about eating. Now that I was reminded, it seemed like a fine idea. Johnnie led me around to the barn, where we unsaddled her horse and gave mine a quart of oats. Mark was waiting on the back porch when we finished.

I hadn't seen Mark since he'd married a girl from Round Rock and moved down there to clerk in a bank. If the MacNally brothers had been a litter of pups, he would have been a different color. He was as tall as Matthew, but with none of his bearlike build and none of the hair-trigger violence that Matthew and Luke shared. He met me with a strong handshake and a big smile.

"Howdy, Bud. Matthew said you'd likely be along, and packing a star, too. Hard to believe. Back when we were kids playing in the bend of the river, I never thought one of us would grow up a lawman."

I agreed. Everybody had expected the MacNally boys to end up outside the law—and Luke was liable to make it yet. As for me, I'd been picked as a farmer, and I'd liked that fine. The weight of the Colt at my hip reminded me just how quickly things could change.

"Supper's ready," Mark was saying as he ushered us inside. " 'Course, I didn't do anything but take it out of the oven. This little lady done all the work." He shot me a wink. "Changed quite a bit from that skinny little thing that used to splash with us in the river, ain't she?"

"Mark! You quit that!"

It was a day for new experiences. I'd never seen Johnnie blush before. Nor had I ever eaten a meal at the MacNally place, and I decided I'd want to try that again. Not having eaten since breakfast probably helped, but the cooking was fine, too. By the time I finished coffee and deep-dish cobbler, I was as full as a Christmas turkey.

"That was a mighty good supper," I told Johnnie. She just looked at me over the rim of her cup. "I surely thank you. I—probably I'd better get along home, now."

"Don't rush, Bud." Mark glanced at Johnnie and grinned. "I was about to turn in myself, but you and Johnnie can visit if you want to."

Johnnie stood up, sudden and graceful as a cat. "I know Bud's tired," she said to Mark, and then she gave me a smile sweet enough to attract honeybees. "I'll help you with your horse."

All the way out to the barn I couldn't help watching Johnnie, the way she walked, the shine of her hair in the lamplight, the stretch of her arms and body when she lifted my bridle off its peg. She turned quickly and caught me at it.

"What's the matter with you? What are you looking at?"

"You." I took a step and got my arms around her. "It really was a fine supper."

She looked up to say something, and I kissed her for the first time since I was twelve years old. Time had improved things a lot. Just for a second, Johnnie's arms slid around my neck and her body pressed into me. Then the surprise wore off and she stiffened.

"Bud, don't. Not while—no."

I let her go, led my horse out into the night, and stepped into the saddle. Johnnie came outside with the lantern. Framed in the wide doorway, she stood looking at me like she couldn't make up her mind whether to run or which way.

"I'm sorry," I said.

"What for? Did you decide it wasn't a good supper after all?"

The wind had laid by the time I started home. I took the shortcut across the ridge to my place, wondering the whole way what it might be like to kiss Johnnie when she wasn't holding back. I'd got so lost in my speculating that Reno was crossing my upper pasture before I thought to wonder who in hell had lit a lamp in my kitchen and built a fire in the grate. Whoever it was hadn't made much effort to sneak up on me. Still, I dismounted to come down to the barn on foot, keeping a careful watch. An old gray horse that I recognized was stabled in the far stall, and someone had already fed the mules. I tended to my horse, then went up to the house.

Pa was at the kitchen table, his knobby hands crooked like a hawk's feet around a cup of coffee. His face in the quiet lamplight looked tired and lined.

"Pa, what's wrong? You've got no business riding around on a night—" I had a terrible thought. "Is Ma all right?"

He gave me a tired smile. "She's fine, son. Just a mite worried. I thought we might want to talk where it was quiet."

He was looking at my waist. I hung my coat on the peg, then took off my holster belt, draping it over the coat so it would be in reach. Pouring myself a cup of the coffee he'd made, I sat down at the table.

"Wasn't dark when I got here, anyway," he said.

He waited to see if I was going to tell him where I'd been. I touched the badge that he'd been looking at.

"Hard to tell ahead of time where this might take me."

He nodded. "I suppose so," he agreed. "But I'm in

a position to tell you where that gun will take you. I've been there."

"Where?"

"To hell."

It sounded like what a brimstone-breathing preacher might have said, but without the least trace of feeling. I remembered Alf Cryer's hint that my pa knew more than his share about killing.

"Pa," I said.

He got up from the table and took two long steps to where I'd left the belt. He drew out the silver Colt, slid it back, then drew it again.

"This holster's no good." His voice was harsh. He shucked the shells out of the cylinder, then threw the pistol out to arm's length, cocking it in the same motion. He let the hammer fall, caught it with his thumb before it snapped, and cocked it again, looking over the sights. "The pistol will do just fine, though. Good balance and a smooth pull. It'll take you there right enough."

"I didn't ask for the job, Pa. Even so, now that I've got it, I don't aim to back away."

He looked at me, a fierce light in his eye. Then he sighed and spun the Colt smoothly back into its holster.

"The job found you," he said. "That's the way of it." Dropping back down on his chair, he folded his gnarled hands on the table. "You don't remember about the war, or what came after."

"Not much." I hadn't been more than three or four when it ended. I could remember being hungry, and that it seemed we were always on the move.

"Probably just as well." Pa rubbed a hand across his face. "Guess I owe it to you to tell this, though. Back then I carried a sidearm by day and slept with it in my hand by night. Natural as eating. When I give back the uniform—such as I had—I kept the pistol. Reckon I would've been scared without it.

"So I wore it—same as many another—hanging smooth and easy by my side when I went home. There was people there, some as didn't fight and some as came in afterward, with money and the military government behind them. They was bent on taking land—for taxes or bad title or any excuse they could find. If they couldn't find one, they'd run you out anyhow."

I stared at him. "I never knew any of that," I said.

"Never meant that you should." He raised his hand as if it held a pistol, then clenched it into a knobby fist. "Some of us fought. There was killing on both sides." He met my eyes squarely. "I did some of it."

"But it was your land."

"Not by the law. Military law." He shook his head. "There was talk of trials and hanging. Your ma and I took you and the girls off by night and ran for Texas. Ran after we got here, too, until I came across Amos Stanton. He's the one that ended it. He sent back word I'd been killed, even had a tombstone set up with my real name on it—your name." He laughed sharply. "I've been dead 'most twenty years. Amos and Alf Cryer know the truth, but nobody else. That's why I've always warned you away from handguns, why I never wanted to see you take to them like I did."

I tried to speak, but my breath was caught in my throat. I wanted to know my real name, and a dozen other things. Most of all, I tried to picture Pa as he'd been then, and I couldn't do it. But I was sure of one thing.

"Where would an empty hand have taken me when Mayberry shot me in the back? What if I'd been unarmed when Ed Willis rode down on me?"

Pa's eyes hadn't left me. "With Willis it was different, son. The first two were forced on you. You waited on Willis and picked your shot. Isn't that how it happened?"

"I don't see your point." I stood up. "I understand why you did what you did. But I've got to do this my own way, and I don't mean to end up buried under a stone with a false name on it."

"All right," he said quietly. "One thing, and salt it away deep: Whatever's happened, you're not a man-killer—not yet."

I thought of Braden. "There's some that would disagree," I said. "Maybe I would, too."

Surprisingly, Pa smiled. "I've seen a few. I reckon I know the signs." Then he put his hand on my arm, and his voice was low and serious. "You weren't born for a killer, Bud, but it's something 'most anybody can learn. You're learning it now, and once you pick it up, it's mighty hard to put it down again."

I didn't answer. After a minute, Pa pushed himself to his feet.

"Well, that's my say. Tomorrow we'll do something about that holster. You've always been a natural marksman, Bud—I seen it from the first. If you're set on this path, maybe I can show you a couple of things to help you stay alive to the end of it."

Chapter 13

THE NEXT MORNING STARTED OFF crisp and clear. We didn't know it at the time, but spring had swept in like a broom to whisk all the cold weather away. I noticed on the way to town that the mesquite were starting to bloom out and the first new green showed in the meadows.

After breakfast I'd done the chores and the milking while Pa worked with a knife and some linseed oil on the old holster. When I came in from setting the milk in the well house to cool he had handed me the gun belt. I strapped it on. Stretched and oiled, shaped so that it fitted the Colt, the holster rode against my right hip like part of me. I tried a practice draw, and the silver pistol came out as fast and deadly as a striking rattler.

Then we went to town. Ma was heartstruck at the sight of me wearing a handgun.

"It goes with the badge," I told her.

"Yes, and look what happened to the last two who

wore that badge!" She clabbered up to cry. "Henry, didn't you speak to him?"

Pa patted her shoulder. "Now, Ruth," he said, "Bud's making his own decisions these days. We don't need to worry about him."

But his look told me he meant to keep right on worrying himself. I mumbled something soothing and headed for the Owl Barber Shop.

"Well, Sheriff Tilden," Homer Moore greeted me. He put aside the broom he'd been using and dusted off a chair. "Don't think I've had the pleasure of serving you before. That sheriff's badge looks mighty good on you. You want to hang your hat and that silver pistol where folks can see them?"

I hung up my hat and coat, then hesitated over unbuckling the gunbelt. "You've taken that as a tool now," Pa had told me on the ride in. "A workman never wants to be far from his tools."

"Guess I'll wear the holster if you don't mind, Homer," I said, easing into the barbering chair. "I need a trim around the edges and a shave—and treat my face as gentle as you can."

Homer chuckled. "Oh, I'll be gentle. Funny, that deputy of yours got the same kind of knocking around you did. It's sure funny how things like that happen."

I gave Homer a hard look and didn't answer. It was plain enough the town talkers had been going over the troubles between me and Braden, and the Lord knew what they'd make of us before they were through.

Homer wrapped a hot towel around my face and spread a sheet over me, still rattling on. "Oh, the town's mighty proud to have you in this job, Sheriff. The good people think mighty highly of the way you handled that Ed Willis, whatever some folks may be saying."

I'd started to ask him what some folks were saying

when the door swung open. "Bud," somebody said. "I've just been looking for you."

With my left hand I turned the towel back. Calvin Hart loomed in the doorway, a big smile on his face. I took my hand away from the butt of the Colt, hoping he hadn't noticed. Calvin was the liveryman and our local horse trader. His business must've been pretty good, because he'd moved about a year before from his old stable near the church to a new livery barn and corral over by the railroad.

"Bud, I've took you at your word," he said. With the habits of a man used to the barn lot, he stamped his feet before he came inside. "You've been talking about starting your own breeding herd. Well, I've picked up the best matched pair of Morgans there ever was—just perfect for you."

"Well, I don't know, Calvin," I said. "Sounds like you're talking about a good deal of money."

Calvin laughed. "Aw, forget the money, Sheriff," he said with a wink. "I figure you're good for it—'specially as long as you keep those bounties coming in on the outlaws you shoot. Just come on down to the corral later and have a look, if Homer don't bleed you too severe."

He was gone before the barber could answer him, but Homer had plenty to say to me while he was spreading lather over my face.

"Oh, the trouble with somebody like Calvin is he ain't never had a good, professional shave. Whiskers like a currycomb! Glad to see you know better, Bud, and I'll expect to see you back regular. You got friends in town, Bud, good friends. You remember that, no matter what some folks say!"

By that time Homer was whisking the razor around under my chin, and I would've agreed with anything. But I was still wondering who "some folks" were when I wandered down to Hart's corral twenty minutes later.

"Here they are, Sheriff." Calvin had seen me coming. "Just putting them through their paces. Ain't they something?"

They were. Tall, heavy, straight-backed, deep brown shading into black, standing quietly like they were just waiting for the harness. Calvin wasn't above stretching the truth a bit when it came to his wares, but this time he hadn't exaggerated. The Morgans made about as neat a matched pair as I'd ever seen.

"Just what you're needing to get a good start. You can breed some fine carriage stock out of them. And I'll set you a price that I wouldn't give to my own mother."

"Calvin, you know my farm doesn't make enough to buy those horses a sack of oats." I ran my hand along the mare's back, watching the way she turned her head to look at me without showing the whites of her eyes. "Pretty well gentled down, aren't they?"

"Gentlest horse in the world! Why, you could let your children play right between their hooves without a minute's fear. And strong? Hitch them up to that locomotive over there and watch them walk away with it."

Now he was exaggerating, and I grinned to show I knew it. My children, he'd said. These horses were good and valuable, fit to pull a carriage for the sheriff's wife to ride in. I walked between the pair to look them over. They were nearly as tall as me.

"Money's no matter between you and me, Bud. I know you're good for it. The sheriff's salary and that reward, that's your business, but I'm prepared to deal with you."

I let Calvin talk along until he got around to mentioning a figure. Then I mentioned a lower one. He complained I was trying to drive him out of business and take the food off his family's table, so I knew I'd hit it pretty close. When he offered to split the difference, it was almost something I could think about.

"That's a lot of money for a country boy," I told him. If Pa had taught me anything besides the wages of wearing a pistol, it was never to make a deal in a fever. "I'll let you know."

"Just as you say, Bud, but don't wait too long. Horses like these will draw a lot of attention."

He was right about that, too. I thought it over all the way down to the sheriff's office. I'd spent some of the reward money from Mayfield, but most of it was still in Banker Shipton's vault. Ed Willis had accumulated eight or ten killings on his soul up in Indian Territory, so the reward for him was a right smart sum—only fair, I decided, since I'd put another killing on mine to collect it. As for the sheriff's salary, I hadn't thought even to ask what it was, and I made up my mind to see Judge Poe before the day was out.

Taking off my coat before settling into Amos Stanton's worn chair, I came across the letter I'd stuck in my pocket the night before. It was signed by some judge in Tennessee, and it recommended Stone Braden to anybody who was interested. The writer said so many nice things that I didn't figure they could all be true of anybody, least of all Braden. I thought maybe the letter had been what Braden had been looking for in the desk, but it didn't matter now. Since Braden was staying on as deputy, he wouldn't need it back right away.

Stuffing the letter back in my coat, I put in an hour or more studying on what a sheriff does. Braden had left a note saying he'd been called out to the Willowby place, and Judge Poe was asking what I proposed to do about delinquent taxes on four ranches in the county. Since I didn't have any idea, I hunted up the fliers on Ed and Sol Willis. I'd promised to put in for Matthew's money, and at least I could do that. When I finished I strolled down to the mercantile.

"It depends on what you want," Todd Milner said. He plunked a big catalog down on the store counter. "Now for you, this farmer's carriage might be the best thing. The top and back seat lift right off, and you've got a flatbed wagon."

"I was looking for something racier."

"Something fitting for your new job, Sheriff?" Todd asked with a grin. "All right, here's a nice rig from Antwerp Wheel Works. Almost like the one Stone ordered."

"That'll do. I'll want shafts and harness for a team. I'm planning to buy that pair of Morgans from Calvin Hart."

Todd pursed his lips in a soundless whistle. "Shoot, Bud, I didn't realize you had the fever, or I'd've shown you something more expensive."

I wished he hadn't put it quite that way. The buggy would be good for training the Morgans and the other stock I had or planned to buy. It was just coincidence I'd picked one a little better than Braden's.

"Half now and half on delivery, that's the usual terms," Todd was saying. "That'll be sixty-seven dollars, cash money. It'll come by rail in about six weeks, same as—"

"I know," I told him. "Same as Stone's."

I paid him, then walked toward the Stanton house. I had some questions for Amos Stanton. The way things were between Ann and me, I wasn't quite sure what I'd say if I ran into her, but it turned out not to be a problem.

"No, Annette isn't home," he said. He was propped up in the bed so that he could see out the window, and he looked a lot stronger. He tugged at his mustache and frowned at me. "I figured you'd know where she was. She said she meant to stop by the office."

"I must have missed her. No matter, it's you I wanted to talk to."

That surprised him a little. He reached down with both hands to adjust one of his legs like it might have been uncomfortable.

"Well, I ain't got much to do but listen, Bud. What's on your mind?"

"I need some advice about sheriffing. It wasn't my idea to take the job, nor to take your place, but now I've got it, I'd like to do it right. Will you help me?"

He blinked, then leaned forward, sounding more like the old Amos Stanton than he had since the shooting. "Why, I'd be right proud to, Bud," he said. "What was it you wanted to know?"

I asked him questions and got answers for the better part of an hour, and then Mrs. Stanton came in and shooed me away, saying I was tiring him. Maybe I was, but he'd sure perked up while he was telling me how to do the work. I promised to come back for another lesson as soon as I could, and then I went back to the courthouse. I stopped by to see Judge Poe, who said it looked like Amos would be indisposed—that was his word—for some time, at least through the next few months.

"We have the greatest confidence in you, my boy," he said, making it sound like "we" meant everybody important in the county. "The greatest confidence."

Then he proceeded to weigh me down with another wagonload of advice, some of it contradicting what Amos had said. I decided to sit down in my office, wait for Braden, and try to sort things out. Just as I came up to the porch, though, I saw a shadow move inside the building. I stopped dead, watching the window and listening hard. I'd left the door locked, but someone was moving around inside. Braden's chestnut horse was nowhere around, so I doubted it was him. Catfooting up to the door, I threw it open, drawing my Colt as I stepped inside.

"Oh!"

Annette Stanton jumped up from the desk like a cat caught raiding the cream pitcher. She was holding the little whiskey bottle I'd found earlier. Her eyes went from my face to the pistol in my hand and back to my face again. I probably looked as surprised as she did, but not half as guilty. Holstering the Colt, I took a step forward and saw that she'd been going through the drawer.

"You're under arrest," I told her, solemn as an owl.

"Bud Tilden!" She'd shaken off her confusion and decided she was angry. "Have you gotten into the habit of drawing that gun on everyone you meet?"

"Only on people I find prowling around in an office I'd left locked. That's dangerous, Ann. I didn't know but what you were somebody robbing the place, or laying to shoot me." I let her think about that, then asked, "What're you looking for? Maybe I can help."

"I . . ." She hesitated, and her eyes slid away from mine. "Papa sent me. There's some things of his here, personal things. He asked me to get them."

Even if I hadn't spoken to her pa, I would've known something was wrong. Annette never could lie for sour apples. "That's good," I said. "I was afraid you'd taken to drink."

She didn't smile. Her face was crimson, and she looked like she was closer to crying. "Bud, I'm sorry.

I want . . ." I waited for her to tell me what she wanted, but she just shook her head.

"Take your time, Ann. I won't get in your way." I thought about leaving again, just letting her look for whatever she was after. Instead, I said, "I ordered a buggy."

She frowned at me like the words didn't make any sense. Then she understood, and she did begin to cry.

"I'm sorry for what I said the other day, Ann. I spoke harsh to you without meaning to."

"And—I hit you," she answered quietly. "I was upset. About Papa and—things. And you were right to think I was seeing so much of Stone."

Considering that I'd seen Johnnie home the night before and kissed her in the bargain, I didn't figure I could throw any rocks.

"Back when we were talking about marrying as soon as we could—" I began.

"Bud, no," she said quickly. "I knew then that I loved you. Now I don't."

"Don't know, or don't love?"

She stood there for what seemed a long time, and now she was looking right into my eyes. "Don't know," she said finally. "I just don't know what's right anymore."

"Let me help."

"Will you give up that gun? And the badge? Will you go back to what you were before?"

There it was. Could I do that, and did I want her bad enough to try? I didn't know the answer.

"I can only be what I am, Ann," I said. "That might be enough, if we're honest with each other."

She wavered, and I even thought she might tell me what she was hiding. But I wasn't somebody she trusted anymore. "I have to go soon," she said. "Please let me finish."

Then I did leave. Walking down those steps from the sheriff's office, I thought back to the way things had been for us that one day in Hart's stable. As I turned down the street, headed no place in particular, I had a good idea how Adam must have felt when the gates of Eden slammed shut behind him.

Chapter 14

OVER THE NEXT MONTH I kept pretty busy. I talked to Ted Willowby, who owned the land that adjoined my farm. He agreed to plant and work my fields on shares for as long as I stayed sheriff. Calvin Hart had insisted that I go ahead and take the two Morgans—Fred and Nell, he called them, the silliest names for working animals I'd ever heard—money or not.

"The horses are yours, Bud. You can pay me when that government money comes in for the Willises," he'd said with a wink. "Just don't try to get away, or I'll have to turn you over to our sheriff!"

Trusting me was pretty good business for him, because it meant I had to feed the horses while we waited for the reward. After running back and forth between town and the farm for a few days, I saw that wasn't going to work. Nights, I still slept in my own house, but I hired Will Stanton to watch the place and tend the stock for me. Will had really grown up following his ride with the posse. He figured it made him a man, and quite a few other folks agreed.

"Sure, Bud, I'll take the job," he told me, reaching out to shake on it. "Don't worry, I'll keep a close eye on things for you." He lowered his voice confidentially. "I'd be glad to do it for nothing after what you done for us, but with Papa down and all, I feel like I need to bring in some money."

"You're not beholden, Will," I said. "I haven't done anything that special."

"Killing Willis, I mean." Will set his jaw like a young bulldog. "I'm still glad you done it. I've made good and sure Stone knows how I feel, too. Don't think I haven't."

"Still see a lot of Braden, do you?"

Will kicked at the ground. "Aw, Bud, he's over to the house 'most every night. You know that." Looking up at me, he added, "He's my friend, too."

"You want to search through my desk?"

"Huh?"

"Never mind."

My personal business settled, I went to being sheriff full time. Without advice from Amos Stanton and Judge Poe I wouldn't have done worth a hoot, but the way it was things rolled along pretty well. Comanche County didn't have any great amount of crime, so I mostly tended to routine duties like mailing tax notices and presiding over county sales and keeping order on Saturday nights when a few cowhands would come in to get drunk. Braden and I even managed to work together when we had to, though he'd been right: My keeping him on as deputy didn't mean we were friends. Whatever burr was under his saddle was stuck tight, and once in a while it made him snort and kick.

There was the time I came into the office one Saturday evening in April. Braden was at the desk, cleaning and reloading his old cap and ball revolver. I remembered the Colt that Matthew had tossed aside the day he'd fitted me with a gun belt. It was hanging on a peg in the gun cabinet. I laid it in front of Braden.

"Why don't you see if this works? It worries me, you carrying that old relic around."

"I'm used to it."

"It's prone to misfire, and mighty slow to reload."

Braden looked me up and down. "I don't figure I'll need to reload," he said, with a trace of his possum grin. "When I come to use it, I'll get the job done."

Well, I'd started out friendly enough. If he wasn't going to have it that way, all right. "Depends on what job you have in mind," I told him. "There's some things a gentleman would be smart not to start. Now, I'm telling you I'd like you to carry something more reliable."

"You've got a point," Braden conceded.

He picked up the Colt and checked it over carefully, loaded it, and seated it in his holster. Then he went to the gun cabinet and took down the county shotgun, a double-barrel stagecoach model ten-gauge. Breaking it open, he thumbed in two loads of buckshot.

"I'd say this ought to be about right—if you don't mind, Sheriff."

"Expecting bank robbers, are you?"

"No." This time Braden's smile was aimed right at me. "I saw what you did to that hawk."

Somebody tapped hesitantly at the office door, and then old Ellis Wheeler stuck his head in the door. "Sheriff?" he said, but I wasn't paying attention to him.

"You're saying it's for me?" I asked Braden.

"Just joking."

"Go ahead and carry it. It's a good backshooter's gun for a gentleman to carry."

That wiped his smile plumb away. "It won't be from behind—nor not with a rifle from so far away nobody could shoot back."

"Sheriff?"

"Then the shotgun won't do you any good."

"Sheriff?" When he was sober, Ellis was the swamper at Finster's Barbary Palace. He wasn't easy in my office except in a cell. "Could I have a word with you?"

It was Braden who answered. "Sure can. I was just going for some supper." He walked out, slamming the door. He took the shotgun with him.

Ellis was staring like an owl in a tree. "I—ah—I didn't mean to bust in on anything, Sheriff."

"Good thing you did. What is it, Ellis?"

"Well, Mr. Finster, he told me, he said to ask you to come over to the Palace—when you have a chance, he said. It's about a man he seen, he said."

"Sure." I reached over to get my hat. If my deputy was outside laying for me, I'd find it out pretty soon. "Let's go see what he's got to say."

Trailing Ellis, I crossed the street and walked up the boardwalk toward the Palace. Birds were twittering in the oaks around the courthouse, and a cold breeze had sprung up, hinting that winter might not be quite finished with us. In their houses, folks were starting to light the lamps and think about supper. There were still people on the streets due to its being Saturday, with folks from the farms and ranches coming in to buy supplies and eat at one of the restaurants and gossip and whatnot. A little later, things might start getting rowdy at Finster's and the other saloons in town, but now everything was quiet as a church. It stayed quiet until we'd turned into the long, dark hall that led into the Barbary Palace. Then somebody let out a whoop, and a gunshot exploded inside the saloon.

I didn't even think. The Colt jumped into my right hand. My left grabbed Ellis by the back of his shirt and shoved him out of the way against the wall. By that time I knew it wasn't me they were shooting at. I heard Finster's angry voice, and then a second shot boomed, followed by a crash. I went fast down the passage, staying against the wall, and came out into the barroom with the silver Colt ready in my hand.

There were maybe twenty people in the place. One table of poker had started up, but the cards disappeared when the dealer saw me, because gambling was against a town ordinance. Over by the bar Finster was arguing with half a dozen spruced-up cowhands. Evidently they'd come in from one of the big spreads up to the north and had started their celebrating a little early. One of them, tall and blond-haired and already a little bit drunk, was still waving a pistol around, though a couple of his friends were urging him to put it away. One of the coal oil lamps that hung at the ends of the bar had been shattered. Glass and the stink of kerosene were everywhere.

Finster caught sight of me. "No trouble, Sheriff," he sang out. "Just a misunderstanding. We're putting it to rights, never fear."

The cowhands looked at me and drew together. Feeling sheepish, I put the Colt away, noticing that the blond cowhand had already holstered his pistol. He still didn't look happy.

"We didn't need no lawman," he grumbled as I came over to talk to Finster. "Hey, Sheriff, why you bothering us? We're just having a little fun."

"Clay's right," another man put in. He was older than the others. "We'll pay for the damage."

"That's fine," I told him. "What suits you and Mr. Finster suits me."

"Yeah," the one called Clay put in loudly. He pushed his way in front of me and stood with his fists on his hips. "So you just tend to your own business, sonny, and don't go spoiling people's fun."

He wasn't that much older than me, but he was a head taller and wide in proportion. That didn't worry me so much as the way his hand kept inching toward his six-gun. I saw his friends starting to move up and wished for Braden and his shotgun.

"I'm not trying to spoil your fun," I said, turning so my hand would be clear if I needed to draw. "I'm just asking you to calm down. I'd hate to have to arrest you."

Clay brayed a drunken laugh. "Well, now, I just expect you would!" His hand was on the butt of his pistol now. He was drunk, but that didn't make him any less dangerous. "Suppose you get yourself out of here, sonny, before I stick that tin star—"

"That's enough, Clay!" The older man hooked his arm and turned him around, and then a couple more moved up to hustle him away. "You fellers just help Clay over to a table and cool him off. Right now." He looked at me. "Sorry, Sheriff. We'll take care of it. You won't have no more trouble out of us—my word on it."

"Thanks."

"Buy you a drink?"

I had my mouth open to refuse, then shrugged.

"Sure."

We moved to the bar, and Finster poured us each a shot of whiskey, disapproving while I drank it. The cowhand passed a couple of remarks about the weather and the cattle, and I answered. Then he touched his hat and went back to the table with the others. I watched him go. I'd never quite turned my back on Clay. That was one mistake I didn't intend to repeat. Clay was a lot paler and more sober than he had been a few minutes before. Two of his friends were talking to him pretty strong, and I caught a word of it now and again.

". . . was I supposed to know? He's just a kid."

". . . knot-headed yahoo, that's Bud Tilden . . . killed nigh a dozen . . ."

". . . shot down both Willis brothers, face to face, and that ain't all . . ."

"Why, he would've killed you in a minute. Did you see those eyes?"

I looked down at the bar, trying hard not to laugh at the way those stories had spread. Then I remembered setting myself while I was talking to him, and how I'd watched for him to move. It hadn't taken any thought to do it—no more than it would have taken to draw the silver Colt and shoot him. By the time Finster came down the bar toward me I didn't see anything funny about it at all.

"Sheriff," Finster said with a nod. He picked up my glass without asking if I wanted another drink. One eye rested on me, troubled, while the other peered off peacefully toward the back of the saloon.

"Did that take care of your problem?" I asked him.

"Oh, those fellers wasn't why I sent for you. They're all right. No, there was another man in here a while ago. I think he was one of the ones with Luke MacNally that day you and Luke had the run-in." He stopped to smile. "The day you bought the rum."

"I remember. What was he doing?"

"Well, nothing. He came in, bought two corked bottles, and left again out the back." His smile faded. "Tell you the truth, I didn't much like his looks, either that day or now. I thought I better tell you."

"Did you see where he went?"

Finster shook his head. "I learnt a long time ago not to follow a man like that into an alley." He thought a minute, frowning. "You'll know him if you see him. Maybe thirty-five, but he's got almost-white hair. Mean eyes, too. Wearing a Montana peak hat and a long duster coat like he's been traveling—and he's carrying a pistol cross-draw fashion."

Coming right down to it, there was no reason why some saddle bum shouldn't ride into Comanche and buy a bottle of whiskey. I hadn't liked the look of Luke's friends, but looking mean wasn't illegal. Still, Finster had been worried enough to tell me, and I was still on edge from my talk with Clay. Braden running around with that shotgun didn't help a lot, either.

"I'll watch for him. Thanks, Finster."

I did better than watch. I took a turn around town, following the advice Amos Stanton had given me about the wisest route. If there was as much as a strange horse on the streets, I didn't find it. I'd about decided that whoever the man was, he'd already ridden on his way. There was another possibility, though. He might have found someplace out of sight for himself and his horse both.

I turned down an alley to come onto Hart's stable from the back. By then it was dark enough so a hunter couldn't have told a buck from a doe. As I stepped across the wire fence into the stable lot a light flared through the cracks in the back door. Somebody had struck a match and probably used it to light a lantern. I took a step toward the door and then another, aiming to get a look through one of the cracks. On my next step, though, my foot caught in a stray piece of wire. It almost spilled me, and in getting my balance I blundered into a sheet of tin that must have been left over from fixing the roof.

About six things happened all at once. The tin fell with a terrible sliding clatter that could've been heard plumb out to my place. The light went out before I could take another step, and then the front door of the stable slammed open like it had been kicked, and two or three horses broke from it at a gallop. I started to run, but then I heard footsteps. Somebody was coming up the alley behind me full tilt.

I spun around, bringing the Colt out and up just as he cleared the fence and started toward me. The hammer came back smoothly, and the muzzle lined up on the shadowy chest so I was sure of my shot. Another half pound of pressure on the trigger—

"Bud! No—don't!"

Somewhere in all the noise and commotion the boyish, changing voice got through to me. The figure skidded to a stop, hands raised, eyes wide in fear and disbelief. I caught the Colt's hammer and dropped it to half cock, stopping myself at the last second from blowing a hole square through young Will Stanton.

Chapter 15

THE SECOND HAND MIGHT HAVE SWEPT all the way around the face of my watch before either of us moved. Then Will's whole body jerked in a shudder. I lowered the Colt and put it away in a hurry, because my hand had started to shake worse than that of an old man with the palsy.

"Will," I said. "Will, damn it all to hell! Don't you know better than to run up behind a man in the dark?"

I was mad because he'd scared me. That wasn't the only reason. I was mad because of what I'd almost done, and I was trying to blame it on him.

Will was close to crying, but he didn't cry. Instead he stuck out his chin and bristled at me.

"Gee-rab-bit! What'd you want to do that for?" He hugged himself with his arms to stop his shivering. "I thought you aimed to kill me, too."

"Too?"

But I knew what he meant. He thought of me as a killer. Maybe all the Stantons did now.

"I'm sorry, Will. I'd never mean to point a gun at you. But you oughtn't to come up in the dark without any warning like that."

That reminded him of something, and for a minute he was the old Will again. "I wouldn't have, except for the horses," he said excitedly.

I'd forgotten all about the horses. "Come on," I told him. We trotted around the stable to the big front doors. A coal oil lantern, still warm, lay on its side near the entrance. I lit it and carried it inside, Will sticking close behind me. Nobody was there, but two of the vacant stalls were standing open. "Did you hear them ride out?"

"No," Will said. "Not those horses. Your horses. The Morgans, Fred and Nell."

I swung around on him, and he flinched back like he expected to be hit. The look on his face told me it would be a long time before he trusted me again.

"What about them?"

"Somebody left the gate down in your back pasture. They're gone."

I bought Will his supper at the restaurant, doing what I could to make him think better of me than he had any reason to. Then I stopped by the office to pick up a rifle and rode home through the dark to my place.

There wasn't any use looking for the Morgans then. I knew that, but I wanted to see for myself that the far gate was down. The gate was just a wire gap in the fence between my property and the MacNallys'. We seldom used it. I kept it wired up tight, so it hadn't just fallen down. But the gate wasn't marked, and I couldn't figure out how anybody could have found it who didn't already know it was there.

When I got to it I found things just the way Will had said. The wire holding the gate had been cut. In the light of a match I saw the big splayed hoofprints where the Morgans had found the gap and wandered over onto MacNally land. There were a lot of other tracks, none of them clear enough to tell anything about at night. I'd have to come back the next morning to round up the Morgans anyway, so I mounted my horse and rode back down to the barn, remembering again how close I'd come to killing Will.

I'd been thinking about that all the way from town. Going over it didn't make it any prettier. I slapped my horse on the neck as I led him through the barn door, which Will had left open in his haste.

"Better be careful, Reno," I told him. "Next thing, I'll be shooting you when you nuzzle up to me."

He whickered and pushed his nose against my shoulder anyway, reminding me it was late and time for some oats. I lit the lantern and turned to unsaddle him. That's when I saw the Morgans waiting calmly by their open stalls. They'd strayed through the gate, had their look around the MacNally place, then come home for supper. I fed them.

"I shut the mules in their stalls," Will had told me between bites of steak at the café. "Then I left the gate down so Fred and Nell could come back if they had a mind to."

At the time, I'd thought that was silly. Now I decided I owed him an extra day's pay.

Next morning before breakfast I rode out with my pliers and a fresh coil of wire. In the early light the tracks made more sense. I found where the Morgans had gone out and come back. Both sets of their tracks covered a set that came through from the MacNally side. I couldn't figure it. Matthew or Mark or Johnnie might have used the gate and welcome, but even Luke knew enough to wire it up again afterward. They had more stock to stray than I did.

While I was wiring the gap closed again I resolved to stop by their place the first chance I got. Mark might know something about it. If not, he'd be interested to hear that somebody had ridden across their place and left the gates down behind him. Satisfied that was all I could do, I had breakfast, saw to the stock, and put in half an hour's practice with the Colt before I started for town again. That was another thing Pa had told me—if a man meant to be good at something, he had to practice.

The day being Sunday, most of the town was at church. I got there late and slipped in at the back. Probably Brother Winslow preached a fine sermon, but I had my own thoughts to think, so I didn't pay a lot of attention. As I was leaving after the service Alf Cryer came up to me.

"Bud," he said, "I'm hoping you'll tell me it's not true."

"All right." I grinned at him. Wearing a celluloid collar and a tie, Alf looked as restless as an old lobo wolf done up in pink ribbons. "What is it that's not true?"

"What your deputy and some others have been spreading all over town—that you drew your gun on Will Stanton last night. That you like to have killed him. I'm hoping you'll tell me that's a lie."

I stopped grinning. Somebody—maybe Will himself—had told the story to Braden, and he'd made sure it got around. Right about then I'd gladly have punched Braden's mouth again, but that wouldn't have helped much. It was my own doing that gave substance to the talk.

Alf was waiting for me to say it was a lie. I shook my head.

"I didn't know it was Will. He came up behind me in the dark."

"Hm." Alf sighed and tugged at his collar. "All right, Bud. How'd a thing like that come to happen?"

"I was looking for a man. I'd just found him at Hart's when Will came running up the alley. I drew before I thought about it. But I didn't shoot."

This time. I thought I could see that in Alf's sharp look, but he didn't say it. Instead, he took out his plug of Star and gnawed off a corner. "Where's the man?" he asked.

"Got away. Rode out fast, him and another." It didn't sound very convincing to me when I said it, and that gave my voice more of an edge than I intended. "A dozen people saw or heard them. Ask around, if you don't believe me."

Alf looked surprised. "I believe you," he assured me. "Them things happen. Best you know, though, that half the old biddies in town, man and woman, are clucking their tongues over it. Likely there'll be some trouble."

"Trouble?" I pulled up short and turned to face Alf. "Let's see if I understand. Folks are mad because I pointed a gun at Will but didn't harm him? The same folks that called me a hero when I shot down Bonner and Mayfield and Willis?"

"Well." Alf worked the cud of tobacco around where it was comfortable and spat thoughtfully. "Well, I wouldn't've put it just that way. Still, I reckon you've got the truth of it."

"Well, they've gotten damn particular all of a sudden."

"You can't blame them so much," Alf said slowly. "It's not the way folks expect you to act."

He was trying to tell me something, but I was too mad to hear him. Had there been any way for me to take back that moment when I'd looked at Will over the sights of the Colt, I'd have done it. But it had happened, and I couldn't change that. The way things lay, I wasn't minded to take a lot of town talk, not even from Alf.

"Folks expect a hell of a lot! Maybe you'd be happier if I'd waited for somebody to shoot me in that alley! Then you'd have Braden for your sheriff, and welcome to him!"

"Bud, you've got no call to talk to me that way."

"No. Nor any right to defend myself, I guess!"

I spun away from Alf, mad enough that I didn't pay much mind to where I was going. The worst thing about it was knowing deep down that he was right. He'd been trying to do me a service, and I'd paid him back by taking all my spite out on him. I'd figured I could count on Alf ahead of most men in town, but now it seemed I'd even wrecked that.

Without my planning it, my steps took me across to Hart's old stable. That's where I'd planned to go anyway, meaning to have a look around in daylight and see if I could learn anything about the men who'd been there the night before. I opened one of the wide doors just far enough for me to slip through, pulling it shut behind me.

Inside, the place was cool and dark, the sunlight squeezing in narrow lines through the cracks between the boards. Jumbled tracks showed in the dust on the floor, nothing I could make head nor tail of. Probably some of the kids had come in to play before Sunday school, wiping out whatever evidence might have been left. I did find one cigarette stub, crudely rolled and smoked down short, but I couldn't be sure if that had been left by the men last night or by one of Brother Winslow's flock slipping in for a smoke before services.

Muttering a curse, I tossed the cigarette away and straightened. I should've known better than to come in. Maybe I'd been expecting Annette to be waiting for me there, up in the loft where we'd come so close to being of the same mind at the same time. Halfway tempted to go and look, I walked to the ladder and rested my hand on a rung. That's when I heard a sudden movement up above, and wisps of dust and hay filtered down from the boards above me.

"Ann?"

As soon as the word was out I knew it couldn't be. I drew back, peering up into the dust-streaked sunlight, alert for a trap. Then I heard a low whisper, too quiet to catch the words, and a smothered giggle in reply.

"Hell," I muttered, and I walked to the door. It seemed like nothing was ever going to be the same again. That one place I'd figured was mine—mine and Ann's—but it looked like somebody else had taken it over, too.

I was in a good mood to be alone, but no sooner did I get outside than Brother Winslow hailed me from the church.

"Bud! Bud, can you come over here a minute?"

I trudged across to the front door of the church building, and he motioned me inside. We were the only two there. Sunlight came in through the stained-glass window behind the pulpit and spread blue and green across the empty pews. I stopped just past the door because it didn't seem right to wear my pistol inside, but I didn't want to take it off. Brother Winslow perched himself on the back of a pew like it was a hitching rail. He had a book in his hand.

"Nice to see you, Bud. I was just marking the hymns for tonight when I noticed you coming out of the stable." He gave me a keen look. "How's the job going?"

"Well enough."

"Good. What takes you to Hart's?"

"Sheriff business." All of a sudden I was disgusted enough to tell somebody about it. "I'm doing a fine job. I missed two men there last night. Then today, I almost blundered onto a couple of kids courting in the loft."

"Were they?" Winslow chuckled. "Well, it's spring. In the spring, a young man's thoughts lightly turn to . . ." He broke off and frowned for a second. "I'm not that young any longer, Bud. You'll have to tell me what they turn to."

I saw his game but didn't want to play. "I wouldn't know," I said. "Mine are on almost shooting Will."

He didn't seem surprised. He put the hymnbook down in the pew and laced his hands over his knee, waiting for me to add something else.

"You knew about that?"

"Oh, yes. I hear about everything, sooner or later."

"What should I do about it?"

"About what? Will?"

"All of it. Will and being sheriff and this gun and Annette—and Braden. Seems like all the trouble started with Braden."

"Does it?" He unlaced his fingers to stroke his beard with one hand. "What do you know about him?"

Looked at straight on, I didn't know much. He'd turned up in Comanche one day with his chestnut horse, looking for a job. He'd made a good impression on just about everybody. Todd thought he'd been a fine clerk and had been sorry when he left to take the deputy's job. Sheriff Stanton had trusted him, and Annette—he'd made a good impression on her, all right. And he'd had it in for me from the start—from the first time he'd seen me, he'd said once. I ran over it in my mind, trying to think what I could've done that day in the store to make us enemies.

"Then there's this." I remembered the letter of recommendation in my coat pocket. I reached it across to the preacher. "This is his pedigree."

Brother Winslow took out his reading glasses and squinted like he was studying scripture. It was nothing more than a few sentences of high-flown southern gentleman's English telling what a fine fellow Braden was, but he carried it over to the light to read it again. Then he folded it up and handed it back.

"I heard you two fought to a standstill," he said.

"Pretty much."

"I hope that'll be enough for you both."

"Not hardly." I looked at the letter in my hand, then back at him. "You sound like you know something I don't."

"I'm thirty years older, Bud. I hope I know *something* you don't."

"If there's anything wrong with Braden, it's my business as sheriff. Is there?"

Brother Winslow resumed his perch on the pew. "That's not what you asked me, Bud," he said. "Do you really want me to tell you what to do?"

I started to answer yes, then thought about it. "No," I said. "You can't do that. Nobody can."

He nodded like I was a bright pupil. "Then I'll tell you something else. The way this all started out, and a lot of it since, it's not your fault."

"I don't—"

"Deputy Johnson's killing, the way you reacted, the way the town reacted, those are all things you didn't control." He waved a hand. "It's like you were a tin can, being kicked along a road, picking up dents but not having much to say about where you went. A man's life can be like that sometimes."

He was going back over part of his morning's sermon that I hadn't heard, only now he was pointing it straight at me.

"The thing is, you've got to decide if you want to keep being kicked along, or if you're going to pick your direction for yourself." He nodded toward the silver Colt at my waist. "It's in you to go either way, Bud. You can make your choices, or you can let that gun choose for you."

Pa had said pretty much the same thing in different words, but neither way made it any easier to see what I needed to do. "Thanks," I said. "I'd better be stopping by the office."

"All right," he said. "One more thing, Bud. Take a day off. Get away and go fishing for a day. It'll do you good."

That struck me as the best piece of advice he'd offered, and I felt pretty good about things, right up until I ran into Widow Mabry on the street.

"The very idea, Bud Tilden!" she greeted me. "Pointing a gun at Will! You should be ashamed!"

After that I hiked on down to the office. The way things had gone, I figured Braden would be there. Sure enough, when I came through the door he was leaned back in the chair with his feet up on the desk. He met me with such a big smile that I knew something else had to be wrong.

"Are you nice and comfortable in my seat?" I asked him.

"Just trying it out for size."

"It won't fit you."

His smile got bigger. "Well, now, we'll see about that," he said.

"What's that mean?"

He stared at me for a second, then laughed. "You really haven't heard yet, have you? Your friend the judge means to call a special election to fill out Amos Stanton's term."

That caught me flat, and I guess it showed. Braden settled back in the chair, grinning at me.

"Hope you don't mind if I run for the office, Sheriff," he said. "After I beat you I can decide whether to keep you on as a deputy or not."

Chapter 16

"IT'S NO REFLECTION ON YOU, BUD. Don't take it that way." Judge Poe fluttered his slender, pale hands to show how upset he was. "Since Amos probably won't ever be able to serve again, a special election is the legal thing to do, that's all."

"That's not what you told me earlier."

"Perhaps you misunderstood. We were all pretty excited that day you brought Willis in dead."

"Perhaps I wasted a lot of time when I could've been working my farm, if you only meant this job to last a month."

The judge sat back and folded his hands on his desk. I hadn't been able to find him on Sunday, so I'd cornered him in his chambers at the courthouse first thing Monday morning. For all the satisfaction I was getting, I might as well not have bothered.

"Now, Bud," he began again, but I interrupted.

"Tell me one thing. How much did Will Stanton have to do with your decision?"

His mouth pulled down at the corners a little. I knew I'd hit my target, but his deep-set eyes never wavered. "Not a bit, Bud. The commissioners aren't swayed by rumors. We're just looking out for the welfare of the county." He gave me a fatherly smile. "Once you're elected fair and square, why, there won't be any question but that the people are behind you. You'll have a much stronger position in office."

"Well, I don't know as I'll even run. I just took this job to accommodate the town. If they don't want me—"

"Now, I'm sure you'll want to think that over, Bud. You've got a week to file." His smile turned sly. "The only candidate we have right now is that deputy of yours. With the name you've made for yourself, you should beat him easily." He stood up and offered his hand. "Glad you came in, Bud. I'll be for you all the way. You just have to understand that my position keeps me from taking sides openly."

"I understand all right."

What I understood was that he didn't mean to be responsible if the rabid wolf he'd appointed as sheriff killed somebody the town didn't want killed. If I won or lost a county election, the voters could blame themselves for the results. I left him with his hand stuck out and stalked away from his office and the courthouse.

I stopped on the boardwalk because I didn't have any good idea which way to turn. Braden would be at the office, and I didn't feel like another squabble with him. Right that minute, two cents would have paid me to turn my back on him and the whole ungrateful county and ride off. I didn't want to be any politician, but the idea of turning the sheriff's office over to a fancy-talking drifter didn't appeal to me either. Considering the way Braden felt about me, living in a county where he wore the badge wasn't likely to be too healthy for one or the other of us.

While I was standing there I gradually started to notice things I'd been too mad to see earlier. The early spring day was as nice as anyone could ask, though I wasn't in a mood for asking. The sky was clear and cloudless, with a smart south breeze tinged with warmth and not cold. Yellow wildflowers were blooming in the pastures along the road from my place. Thinking about them, I remembered what Brother Winslow had said. Maybe he was right, and what I needed was a day away from the sheriff's job and the whole affair. I had plenty to think about, and I'd never been able to think as well with a lot of people around.

Turning the idea over in my mind, I strolled toward the sheriff's office. By the time I got there I'd made up my mind. Braden was at the table beside the gun cabinet. He had the county's shotgun broken down, and he was drawing a cleaning rod through one of the barrels.

"Aren't you afraid I'll slip up on you while you're not fixed to shoot?" I asked.

"Figured I'd be safe this one time," he said with a grin. Sometimes he could act almost bearable. Then he remembered who I was, and his grin turned nasty. "Guess you're ready to start your campaign?"

I grinned back at him. "You campaign," I told him. "I'm going fishing."

The place I'd picked was a bend of the river where both banks were MacNally land. All of us had fished and swum there since we were kids, so I didn't think I needed to ask their leave. Well back from the water I stopped the wagon and unhitched the mules, picketing them to graze on the river grass. I'd been neglecting them lately. I had thought of bringing Fred and Nell, but they were too fine a team to put in front of a farm wagon. If I kept the sheriff's job—and now that meant if I stood for election and beat Braden—I'd have to find somebody to work the stock for me.

It was midmorning by the time I baited my hook with a freshly dug worm. Out in the channel the river ran clear and swiftly from the spring freshets. I dropped the hook closer in, where the water eddied in lazy swirls, and settled down to blend into the scenery. A blue jay skittered past so near I could've touched him with the pole, two red finches in furious pursuit. Fifty yards down a gray fox put his head out of the brush, studied me, then minced over to lap up a drink. Just as quickly he was gone. Watching him while the sun got into my bones, I decided Brother Winslow's advice had been right. I'd been so tied up in my own troubles that I was forgetting some of the best parts about living. Only the weight of the holstered Colt reminded me that those troubles hadn't gone away.

I horsed the bait along toward the edge of the channel, knowing there was a rock ledge just beyond. In a second the current would take it over, and a big catfish—

It didn't get there. Something grabbed onto it and started upstream. By the time I realized I had a bite the line was fairly sizzling along. I yanked to set the hook, and the water exploded into foam and glimpses of scaly green.

"Got you," I muttered, and I started hauling back on the pole. It arched double. I eased off just short of breaking strain. "All right, let's try it this way."

Moving slowly along the bank, I guided the fish toward the shallows. He didn't like that either. At the last minute he made another run for the channel, almost spilling me on the slick bank.

"Nice try," I told him. "Now let's see if you can break this line."

I started backing away from the river, gradually lifting the tip of the pole against the fish's strength. He came back to the shallows, fighting me all the way. Just one good tug short of the bank he lunged out of the water, shaking his head like a bull. I had time to see he was an old green-backed bass who must have been living there for years, and then the line went slack, and he drove for the channel with a powerful sweep of his tail.

I pulled in the broken line. It had snapped just above the hook. My own fault. I never should have dared him. And I should've checked my tackle before I started. The line was old and rotten, and I realized how much time had passed since I'd last been fishing.

After that I strung on a fresh line and caught a nice mess of sunfish, then two eating-size cats from the edge of the channel. That put it past lunchtime. I left the fish and built up a little fire. While it was burning down to coals I baited a hook with an old chicken liver and cast it out into the swift water of the channel. Tying the heavy line off to the trunk of a willow sapling at the water's edge, I washed my hands and squatted to unstring and clean a half dozen of the sunfish. Night would have been a better time to put out a trotline, but I couldn't afford to stay that long. Besides, I didn't know when catfish were hungry and when they were sleepy.

I knew when I was sleepy, though. I fried up the sunfish with a little cornmeal and ate them hot from the skillet while my grounds were bubbling in the coffeepot. Then I sat on the tailboard of the wagon with a big tin cup of fresh coffee and looked off to the east through the trees toward Comanche. All I could see was trees. The road was out of sight, curving beyond the ridge someplace. Except for my wagon and the mules, the world might have been fresh-made, with nobody in it yet except me. I grinned at that idea and took an old gum blanket from the wagon, spreading it on the open, grassy bank of the river.

Maybe because I hadn't been sleeping much I fell right into a dark well. For once I didn't have any dreams, no silent rider creeping up on my blind side. Chances are I'd be there still but for a big splash that brought me awake and up on my knees, wondering if I'd really heard it.

I'd slept the afternoon away, and it was near sunset. At first everything looked just the same, the clearing and my wagon and the browsing mules. Finally I noticed that the little willow sprig where I'd tied off my trotline was gone—limbs, trunk, roots, and all. A trail of moist dirt led from a ragged hole down to the riverbank. I was trying to figure out what had happened when the willow popped up with a swish out in the middle of the river. It hung there, jerking and fighting the current like it was alive.

I ran to get a rope from the wagon. Either somebody had hitched a team to the willow and dragged it out there, or I'd hooked into the grandfather of channel catfish, a fish that could have carried Jonah to Nineveh. I made a cast with the rope, came up short, and tried again. That time was even shorter. If I wanted that fish, I'd have to go in after him.

Tying one end of the rope around a pecan trunk no fish could uproot, I shucked off my boots and clothing, laying my gun belt on top of the pile. The water was cold enough to shrink a man two or three sizes. Now that the sun was off the river, it didn't seem nearly so much like spring. By the time I reached the floating willow I was beginning to doubt the whole idea of swimming out. I threw a hitch around the trunk of the willow and started for shore, figuring to get into my pants and then let one of the mules haul the line out. Just as I started up over the rock ledge a woman's voice called, "Bud? Is that you trespassing?"

I dropped back into deeper water, paddling to stay in place. Johnnie MacNally was up on the bank above me, hands on her hips. In her work jeans and denim jacket she looked lean and wiry as any young cowhand, and it was hard to picture her in that blue dress.

"Who did you mistake me for?" I asked her.

"Well, it's been a while since I've seen you like that. Are you all right?

"Fine."

"Not cold?"

"Not now."

"Swimming?"

"Fishing."

"Oh." Her eyes followed the rope from the bank. "You've caught a nice tree."

"If you'd lead one of the mules down, I'll show you what's on the end of that line—after I get dressed."

She took hold of the rope. The willow wasn't fighting the current any more. It had swept down until it had a straight pull from shore, and it bobbed easily when Johnnie tugged on the line.

"I don't think we'll need a mule."

"Damn," I muttered, and I swam toward the willow. Johnnie was drawing it back toward shallow water. I got hold of it and felt along the trunk. The slick bark was cut and skinned where the line had worked against it, but the line was gone. Now I had two fish stories, and nobody was likely to believe either of them. "Twice in one day!"

I let go of the willow, and Johnnie eased it up into the shallows. "There," she said. "It's a good thing I came along, or you might have lost your tree."

Thinking about the catfish I'd never see, I wanted to reach up and pull her in. Instead, I got to laughing so hard I lost my breath. Johnnie stared down at me in concern while I coughed and sputtered, and that seemed even funnier. Finally I caught myself up enough to ask, "What are you doing here this time of day?"

"Helping you."

"Thanks."

She looked off across the river. "I came for a swim. A bath." Then she smiled. "From the looks of your goose bumps, it may still be a little cold, though."

"Water's fine," I said. "Come on in. Don't let me stop you."

At first she didn't answer. She was still smiling, but her eyes had a serious look. "We did that once," she said. "Remember? We were twelve."

"You were twelve." It's funny how seldom a fellow thinks about the best times of his life. "I was thirteen."

"I don't think you really wanted me to then," she said. "Either," she added softly.

She was fishing, too, but I wasn't sure what she wanted. I knew what I wanted to tell her, though.

"Sure I did. I do now."

"Serious and true, Bud?"

"Serious and true."

She opened her shirt at the collar, then undid a couple more buttons. My throat tightened up as I waited. I'd forgotten the coldness of the river and the tug of the current against me, everything but Johnnie. She hesitated, looking back through the trees.

"What if somebody comes?"

"We'll tell him we're married."

She laughed at that. "No, what if it's someone we know?"

"Then we'll have to *get* married." I prayed for her to hurry before the light was gone. "Dare you," I added.

When she was twelve she'd never turned down a dare. She studied my eyes for a moment longer, making up her mind about something. Then she nodded quickly and slipped back out of sight into the brush along the bank. I thought she'd gone until I saw her shadow glide out into the water downstream, sleek and quick as the fox had been. She swam toward me with a long, graceful stroke, stopping just a few feet short to stand in the shoulder-deep water.

"You told me it wasn't cold!" she accused.

"I'm not cold."

I moved toward her, but she pulled back quickly, eyes shy as a deer's. Her bare shoulders glistened in the fading light, and her loosened black hair trailed back behind her.

"Bud, are you sure?"

I wasn't sure of much of anything just then, least of all what she expected me to say. I'd have given my team of Morgans to know just the answer she wanted. Instead, I turned the question back on her.

"Are *you* sure?"

"I always have been," she said, so quietly I almost didn't hear over the rush of the current. 'I never meant to tell you, until—" She stopped suddenly and shook her head, her hair spreading like a fan on the surface of the water. "Never mind. What I mean is I love you, Bud. Right down to the ground."

"Johnnie." I reached out, and this time she didn't back away. She came to me, ready to be kissed, our bodies just brushing together under their cool covering of water.

That's when we heard the sound of a horse's hooves

in the gravel. Downstream on the far bank a man dismounted and walked to the water's edge, turning his head slowly this way and that. He wore a long white duster coat that stood out like a ghost against the dark trees, and even from where I was I could see he was carrying a rifle.

Chapter 17

MY FIRST THOUGHT was that I could've shot the intruder dead for interrupting just at that moment and never felt a twinge of conscience for it. My second was what a fool I'd been for leaving the Colt out of reach on the bank. Whatever had gotten me to pretending I was in the Garden of Eden, the stranger's presence reminded it wasn't so.

Probably he'd heard our voices just as he dismounted and now was trying to find where the sound had come from. He turned our way, raising his head in the twilight like a coyote sniffing at the wind. Johnnie caught her breath sharply and started to pull away, but I held her close against my side.

"No. Don't move. He can't see us."

I hoped I was right. He was in the open, standing in what remained of the light. We were deep in the shadows of the bank. From where he stood our heads should've been just a darker spot against the darkness behind us. He waited what seemed a long time. Beside me Johnnie began to shiver, biting her lip to stop her teeth from chattering. Then one of my mules must have caught the scent of the strange horse. He brayed and came clopping down to the bank for a closer look. The man jerked his rifle up, then cursed savagely, loud enough to carry across the water. Stalking back to his horse, he slammed the rifle into its boot, then took a wooden bucket from the saddle horn. Still growling in his beard, he knelt to fill the bucket, then mounted and rode back up the slope.

Modest or not, I scrambled up the bank and over to where I'd left clothes and gun belt. I got the Colt first, then struggled into my jeans. The air was a lot colder than the water had been, but I was hot all over from anger at the fix I'd put myself and Johnnie into. Pa, and Matthew before him, had warned me how it would be once I'd picked up a gun. Maybe I should've known from the start, but this was the first time I'd really understood what they had meant.

"Johnnie?"

"I'm here, Bud." She came from the bushes already dressed. "I have to go."

"No." I went to her. She was still shivering. I put my arms around her and pulled her tightly against me. "I have some blankets in the wagon. Wrap one around you while I build up the fire."

"Bud, no, I—"

I kissed her. At first she held back, but then she put her arms around my waist and just seemed to melt against me. I felt like I was back in the river, the current sweeping me deeper and deeper under the smooth surface until I was ready to drown. Finally Johnnie pulled her mouth away and buried her face against my shoulder.

"Stay," I said.

I felt her head shake. "I can't. Mark. He'll be

worried." She lifted her face and looked at me. "He's leaving tomorrow. Please, Bud."

"That man. Who was he?"

"I—don't know."

"He was on your land."

Johnnie put her head down and pressed into me again. "I don't—he's probably a drifter, just passing through," she said. "We—I have to go."

"Do you want to?"

Her whisper was so soft I could barely hear it.

"No."

I drew a long breath and opened my arms. For a moment longer she stood there, then she stretched on tiptoe and kissed me quickly. By the time I could reach for her again she was running for the place where the roan was tied. She swung lightly up into the saddle and reined the animal around, stopping to look at me.

"There'll be another time for us, Bud—if you're sure."

Without waiting for an answer she turned the roan and rode away into the dark. I went back to get my shirt. The weight of the sheriff's star reminded me of the job and Braden and what I'd come there to decide. The way things had turned out, I hadn't spent a lot of time thinking about it. Even so, looking back the way Johnnie had gone, I found that I'd made up my mind just the same.

As soon as Judge Poe reached his chambers next morning I was there to fill out the papers that said I was officially running for sheriff. He'd set the election for the second of June, barely a month away. It wasn't much time for campaigning, but I figured that would work in my favor. I'd grown up in Comanche County, and almost everybody knew me. For all his winning ways, Braden was still an outsider.

I was in a pretty good mood when I headed for the office to give my deputy the good news. Braden wasn't there, but Alf Cryer was. In fact, he was at the head of about a dozen men who had gathered on the office porch like crows on a clothesline. They sort of bunched together when they saw me coming, and for a second I felt like a fox dumped out before a pack of hounds.

"Morning, Alf," I said. "Any trouble?"

"That depends." Alf looked solemn. "Me and these fellers"—he gestured at the group behind him—"we're a sort of committee. We wanted to talk to you."

I looked at the others. They were all men I knew, and most of them I considered friends. Todd Milner grinned from behind Alf, while Calvin Hart looked uncomfortable. Even Seth Crabtree had pried himself away from his bottle to stand at the back, preening himself like the whole thing was his idea.

"I'm always proud to talk to you all, Alf. Let me unlock the door and I'll brew up a fresh pot of coffee."

"That deputy of yours ain't here," Alf said. "Out campaigning, I'll bet. You ought to keep him busy in the office so he won't have time to run around behind your back."

"He's on county business," I told him. Truth to tell, I didn't know where Braden was. He'd given me no cause to complain about the way he did his job, though, so I owed it to him to say so. "Besides, he's running for sheriff. He has a right to campaign."

I got the door open, and everybody trooped inside behind me. Braden had left a note on the desk and a pot of coffee on the stove lid. I took my chair while the others were finding cups.

"That's why we're here, Bud," Todd said when everybody was settled. "We know he's running. How about you?"

Seth Crabtree cackled a laugh. "Don't worry. Bud ain't going to let that yahoo take his girl and his job both. Are you, Bud?"

I turned toward him, but Alf stepped forward quickly. "Anyways, Bud, we want one of our own for sheriff—a man we know about," he said. "We're here to ask you to go sign up for the election."

Looking from one of them to the other, I had a little trouble answering. It had been quite a spell since anybody had gone out of his way to show me I still had friends—anybody except Johnnie, at least. They all looked so serious that I couldn't help but smile.

"I'd like to oblige you, Alf," I said, "but the fact is, I can't sign up now." He started to argue, but I stopped him. "I already did sign up, just before I came over here. Hope I can count on all your votes."

Alf broke into a big grin. "You bet you can! Just happens we brought along something to show how we feel." He motioned to somebody in the group. "Bring it out, Hector, so he can try it."

I hadn't noticed Hector Ramirez. Hector ran the saddlery and made boots and the like on the side. He was a short, slender man, so shy he could just disappear in a crowd. He came forward reluctantly, taking something from a bag he'd brought with him.

"Try this on, Bud. You must take off the old one."

"This" was a wide gun belt, the leather new and fresh-smelling. Hector had tooled flowers and winding vines all around the cartridge loops. At the back he'd tooled BUD in big letters. I held still while Hector wrapped it around me and measured, then punched a hole for the buckle.

"There you go!" Crabtree brayed. "That's how a sheriff ought to look, Bud."

I shifted the belt to settle it over my hips. After the one I was used to it felt stiff and strange, but it was a pretty thing. I tried the silver Colt in the holster and shook my head.

"I thank you, and I'll be proud to wear it," I said. "But I'd better keep my old holster on it."

"But that won't match," Todd protested.

Alf Cryer understood. "No, but it fits that long pistol mighty well," he said. He winked at me. "Wouldn't be surprised if whoever fixed it up really knew his business."

They stayed a little longer, and then we all shook hands, and everybody went about his own business. Alf lagged behind the others.

"What you ought to do, Bud, is go see Sheriff Stanton. Get him on your side. His word carries a lot of weight."

It didn't seem likely I'd ever get any of the Stantons on my side again, but I didn't say so. "I don't know, Alf. I figure folks will make up their own minds."

"Well, think about it. It could mean a lot to you."

"I'll think about it."

During the day I did think about Alf's suggestion. According to the note, Braden had ridden over to Sipe Springs to serve some papers in a lawsuit. When I came to consider it, Braden had spent a lot of time circulating around the county, while I'd stuck pretty close to the office. There was nothing wrong with that, but it meant that a lot of people had gotten used to seeing him with a badge. Maybe he'd been campaigning all along, and I just hadn't noticed. The visit from Alf and the rest showed I had supporters, too, but I wondered if Braden was going to be quite as easy to beat as I'd thought.

Enough work had stacked up while I was on my holiday that I stayed busy until along in the afternoon. When I found a good place to stop I got my hat, settled the new gun belt around my waist, and walked down to the Stanton house. I was surprised to find Amos Stanton out on the porch, sitting on the wide swing where Annette and I had quarreled. When he saw me he reached across for two stout sticks. Leaning heavily on them, he heaved himself to his feet.

"Sher—Amos!" I said. "It's good to see you up. Nobody told me you were walking."

He smiled, then lowered himself carefully to the swing again. His face was coated with sweat from the effort, but I could see he was pleased at having surprised me.

"Not walking much. Not yet, anyway." He was thinner than he'd been, and still gray-faced from being cooped up, but he looked a lot better than the last time I'd seen him. He punched one of his legs like it belonged to somebody else. "Feeling's coming back, but it's pretty slow. Doc won't make any promises." He turned his faded blue eyes on me. "Been a while since you've come around. I guess you figure you've learned all there is about being sheriff?"

"No, sir. But I have been busy."

He nodded. "People still tell me things," he said. "I hear you've been doing a good job."

"That's what I'm here about. The job. I've decided to run against Braden to see if I can keep it. I'd appreciate your support."

"I see." He leaned back in the swing and tugged thoughtfully at his mustache. For a minute he didn't say anything. Then he shook his head regretfully.

"No, Bud. I can't endorse you, if that's what you want."

Well, that was about what I'd expected. I just hadn't known it would feel quite so much like a slap in the face.

"All right. I know how much you think of Braden."

He shook his head again. "I don't intend to take his side either," he said. "We have to let the people choose. I can't take sides between you and Stone. That's all."

"Oh. Is it something personal against me?"

He frowned a little. "Not personal, no," he said slowly. His eyes went to the fancy gun belt Hector had made me. "You might've made a good lawman, Bud. You might yet. But I've known of a lot of men who've taken to the gun the way you have, and I've never seen it end but one way."

Probably that was what he'd told Annette, too. Looking at him, I couldn't see that his way had turned out a lot better. I hadn't come there to argue, though.

"We'll see," I told him. "Thanks for your time."

"If you want to see Annette—"

"Not just now. Thanks."

After that I walked to Milner's store to pick up my mail. Will Stanton was inside, over by the case where Todd kept the guns and ammunition. He'd just paid for something when I came up.

"Hello, Will," I said. "How was school?"

He glanced at me quickly and palmed the box like a cardsharp. "Not bad," he said. "I was just getting ready to go out to your place for the chores."

"No hurry."

"Don't worry, I'll get it done."

He shoved the box in his pocket and went out like

he'd been caught in the cookie jar. Todd Milner looked puzzled.

"What's wrong with him?"

"No telling. I'm not having much luck with Stantons lately." Todd didn't know whether to laugh or not, so I asked, "What was he buying?"

"Percussion caps. Wonder what use he's got for them."

Thinking of the old cap and ball revolver Braden had given up, I had a pretty good idea. I asked for my mail, passed the time with Todd a few minutes longer, then headed back for the office.

Besides a fresh bundle of wanted posters, there were two long envelopes. One held a draft for the reward on Ed Willis, made out to me. The other was Matthew MacNally's reward for Sol. I spent a few minutes figuring, decided I could make a payment on the farm to Pa, pay most of what I owed Calvin for the team of Morgans, and have enough left over to cover the last installment when my buggy came in. Thinking about the buggy, I lifted the other draft. Matthew probably wasn't home yet, but Johnnie would be. Going out to deliver Matthew's mail suddenly seemed like the best idea I'd had all day.

I got Reno from Hart's old stable, where I'd been keeping him, and rode out, cantering until I was past the Stanton house and then giving him his head. He was eager to run after standing in a stall all day. I didn't mind a bit. Johnnie and I had left a few questions unanswered the day before, and I was looking forward to talking about them a little more.

When I reached the MacNally place no one was there. Johnnie had told me Mark would be going home to Round Rock, which probably meant Matthew would be back soon. I grinned, remembering the warning he'd given me about dealing lightly with Johnnie's affections. That wasn't exactly what I had in mind, but I didn't know how he would see it. The question didn't worry me much as I went around to check the barn.

A big brindled dog came out and barked at me, but that was all the interest I provoked. Johnnie's little roan was nowhere in sight. If she'd ridden into town, we should have passed on the road, so I decided she must have gone the other way. More disappointed than I would've guessed, I left a scribbled note in the screen door and started back for town.

I took the shortcut over the ridge to my place, mainly because it passed close to the bend where Johnnie and I had swum the day before. Along the crest I paused. The river showed through the trees below me, but the bend was farther down and out of sight. From somewhere near it a thin column of smoke rose into the clear sky. I frowned at the smoke. Nobody lived over that way; it was all MacNally land. Somebody was camped there now, though—maybe the same man who'd come to the river for water. Maybe the one who'd used the gate in my back pasture. Whoever was there, I decided it was my business to meet him.

Leaving the road, I angled back through the woods. Not far below the bend the river ran into broad shallows where I could cross without getting too wet. Two hundred yards below, smoke rose from the stovepipe of a line shack the MacNallys hadn't used for years. I tied Reno in the brush, slipped my rifle out of the saddle boot, and worked toward the front of the cabin. Three horses stood outside the cabin. One of them I'd never seen before, but the second had been across the river from me the night before. The third was Johnnie MacNally's roan, still saddled and with its coat dark from sweat.

Johnnie's was the first voice I heard when I neared the door. "I won't have it," she was saying. "You'll get out of here today—right now."

A man laughed. Chair legs scraped on the wooden floor. "We'll be going, right enough," he said. "We was crazy to stay this long."

"Right now," Johnnie repeated. "Without Luke."

"Well, now," the man said. "I don't know as I could get used to traveling without a MacNally with us."

I stepped cautiously onto the sagging porch just as a second man spoke.

"What the hell, Shirey?" His voice was a resentful whine. "Every time we need Luke, he's drunk. Let's saddle and ride."

"Just what I had in mind," the one called Shirey said. He laughed again. "And I thought we'd invite little missy here to ride along."

Johnnie said, "You stay away from me." But all the assurance was gone from her voice. It came to me I'd never heard her sound scared before.

"You're crazy," the other man said. "They'd hang us for that quicker than—"

"Shut up. Besides, you can't tell—she might like it. You go saddle the horses while missy and me talk it over. Give us about half an hour."

There was the sound of rapid movement, then a sharp cry from Johnnie.

"No, you don't, girly. That's better."

"Shirey—"

"Get along, I said! Maybe you can have a turn later."

I was ready when the door opened. A man came through, most of his attention still back over his shoulder. He was lean and unshaven, and I had time to recognize him as the one who'd filled his bucket at the river. His mournful face twisted into a comic expression of surprise and fear when he turned and saw me. He went for the pistol at his belt, but I was already swinging the barrel of my Winchester at his head. It caught him with a solid crack alongside the jaw, and he went down like he didn't have any bones.

In the second that took I could hear what was going on inside the cabin. "Bitch!" Shirey had yelled, followed by the crack of a slap and the sound of ripping cloth. I stepped across the man on the porch, levering a shell into my rifle as I came through the door.

Shirey froze at the sound. It couldn't have been for long, but long enough for me to see every detail. Johnnie was twisting desperately in his grip. A red patch across her cheekbone was quickly swelling into blue. One of Shirey's hands, the one twisted in her hair, was bleeding from a bite. With the other he was just throwing aside most of her checked work shirt.

"Move away," I said.

He turned to look at me, just his head. Finster had given me a good description of him, from the dirty-white hair to the wide-set snake's eyes. The eyes widened in surprise, then narrowed when he saw the badge on my shirt.

"This ain't what you think, Sheriff. Me and—"

"Move away." It was like somebody else speaking with my voice. "Or I'll kill you this second."

He swallowed, then slowly relaxed his hold on Johnnie. She flung herself to the other side of the room, her hands trying to pull together what was left of her shirt. Shirey stepped back toward the wall, letting the flap of fabric drop from his hand. He was wearing a pistol, and I waited for him to make a move toward it. If it had been a praying time, I'd have prayed that he would.

"No!" Except for the ugly bruise, Johnnie's face had gone dead white. "No, Bud! Don't kill him!"

I didn't look away from Shirey. "Why not?" I asked her.

"Please, Bud! You have to let them go!"

I started to ask why, but I already knew. It was the same reason she'd let Mark start home without telling him about Shirey and the other one. She was looking after her brothers. She hadn't wanted Mark to tackle them alone. She didn't want either of them testifying in court because of what they might say about Luke. I couldn't see that they'd be such a problem dead, so I waited another minute to see if Shirey might reach for the gun.

Finally, he grinned. "You'll have to shoot me cold, Sheriff," he said. "I ain't going to give you any more excuse."

I walked up against him until the muzzle of the Winchester punched him in the chest. Beads of sweat came out on his forehead, but he didn't move. With my left hand I jerked his gun out of its holster and tossed it across the room. He cursed me. Still holding the rifle on him, I lifted my boot and smashed the heel down on his instep the way I'd kill a snake. Something snapped, and he fell back against the wall with a strangled scream.

"You've broke it!" He slid to the floor and clutched at his foot. "God damn you, you've broke my foot!"

"Very likely," I told him. "Sit still or I'll break the other one."

Behind me the second man stirred. He had hold of the door frame and was trying to pull himself up when I took his gun. He didn't seem to notice. The side of his face was swelled up like he'd tangled with a swarm of bees. He shook his head and spat out a cupful of blood, then slumped back down again.

Still true to what I'd learned from being shot, I hadn't turned my back on Shirey. He evidently didn't have a hideout gun as I'd hoped, but he did try to get up and lunge on one foot toward where I'd tossed his pistol. I took a long step to kick his good leg out from under him. He fell with a crash that shook the whole cabin and lay there moaning.

"Get up." I nudged him with my boot hard enough so he'd notice. "Since you're so anxious to move around, get outside and saddle your horses."

"Damn you!" Shirey rolled to his knees, clutching his arms across his middle. "My ribs. When you knocked me over. I can't saddle no horse. I can't even walk."

"Crawl."

He raised his head. His mouth twisted into a snarl, and he started to say something else. I rested the muzzle of the Winchester right between the pale, snaky eyes.

"Don't talk. Move."

"Bud—" Johnnie began, but I wasn't in a mood to listen. Whatever devil had been tugging at my coattails had me by the throat now.

"Hush. I'm busy." To Shirey, I said, "Your choice. Want to bet I won't shoot you right here?"

Cursing wearily, he dragged himself across the splintered floor and out on the porch. I followed him. On the way I grabbed the collar of his friend's coat and dragged him along. He still wasn't taking much interest in things. Johnnie brought up the rear, staring at me all the while with the rabid-wolf expression I'd come to know so well.

Shirey made slow work of the saddling and bridling, but with a little encouragement he managed it. Then I had him heave his friend into the saddle and mount up himself. I'd taken their rifles and checked through their saddlebags. I knew they wouldn't be long rearming themselves, but that would hold them for the moment.

"I ain't forgetting this," Shirey said. The other one didn't say anything. He looked too sick.

"See that you don't," I said. "You'd better remember, because the next time I see either one of you I'll shoot you down and let you lie. Now ride out of this county and don't ever set foot here again. And thank the young lady that you're in that saddle and not across it."

Shirey might have answered, but I couldn't hear if he did for the hammering of my heart. He rode out like he'd taken my meaning, leading the horse of the second man. I watched them go, still fighting the urge to raise the rifle and knock them off their horses. When they were out of sight I finally realized Johnnie had been pulling at my arm.

". . . enemies that'll dog you from now on," she was saying. "You humiliated them. What got into you?"

"The devil," I murmured.

She looked at me like she believed it. "Bud? Are you all right?"

"Fine."

I turned toward her. Her color was coming back. It was like I'd never really seen her before. Her face reminded me of the angel in the stained-glass window of the church.

"Bud?"

"You were nice," I told her. "At the river. You're even nicer in daylight."

She blushed scarlet and held her arms across her ruined shirt. I walked back to the cabin and found a blanket. Coming back to her, I put it around her shoulders, then used it to pull her close to me.

"Bud, listen. I need your help."

I put my arms around her. "All right."

"No, with Luke. Listen to me! Matthew's not back yet. You have to do something about Luke!"

I blinked a couple of times, then drew a deep breath and felt the demon let go. Johnnie was straining away from me. I loosened my hold but kept my hands on her shoulders.

"What about Luke?"

"He was with them. They sent him into town for supplies and a bottle. He hasn't come back yet. Probably he's still at Finster's Palace."

"What do you want me to do?"

"Arrest him."

It was my turn to stare at her. "Has Luke got himself on a poster?" I demanded.

"Not yet. Not that I know of." Johnnie shook her head. She hadn't cried from anything that had happened to her, but she was close to it now. "But he will! I'm afraid he'll do something awful unless you can hold him until Matthew gets home."

"I drew her to me again. "If Luke's at Finster's, he'll keep," I said, nuzzling at her hair.

"What if he comes across your deputy?"

"That might save us both a lot of trouble," I said. "Anyway, Braden hasn't any reason to be interested in Luke."

She shook her head. "I'm afraid Luke might start shooting if he sees a badge. Any badge."

That might still save me some trouble, I thought, but I didn't put it into words. Instead, I laughed. "That's a comfort," I said. "Don't go out of your way to cheer me up."

Johnnie looked closely at me for a minute, and then she joined in my laugh.

"I'm glad I know you again," she said. "For a while

there I didn't. The way you treated those men . . ." She broke off and shivered.

"I'm me now," I said. Doubt still showed in her eyes, so I put both my hands behind me and leaned forward to brush her mouth with mine. I kissed her softly until she slipped her arms around my neck. When we broke apart she looked at me seriously.

"Why, Bud? Why did you act like that?"

I looked at her torn shirt and her bruised face. "They left my gate down," I said.

Chapter 18

NOT WANTING TO LEAVE JOHNNIE ALONE, I rode back to the house with her and snacked in the kitchen while she put on a fresh shirt. Then we headed for town to corral Luke MacNally before he got around to killing Braden. I had trouble keeping up my enthusiasm.

We left our horses in Hart's stable. Shirey and his partner had found it a good place to keep out of sight, and I figured it would work as well for me. It was my plan that Johnnie wait across the street in the church while I looked for Luke. She dug in her heels at that.

"I'm going with you."

"Not into Finster's. Besides, if there's going to be shooting, I don't want you in the middle of it."

"Listen here, Bud—"

"You listen. I've got six empty cells over at the county jail, and I'll sling you into one if I have to. That's your choice—Brother Winslow's church or my jail."

Her expression suggested I'd live to regret that, but finally she nodded.

"All right. I'll stay at the church."

"Cross your heart?"

She made a face at me but went through with the childhood ritual. "Satisfied?"

"No, but we'll talk about that later. Right now I have to find Luke."

A lantern still burned in the sheriff's office. I found Braden propped on one of the cots in the first cell. He was dozing over a book. When he heard the door open he shook himself awake and reached down for the shotgun that was on the floor beside the bed.

"You'll need your boots, too," I told him.

He sat up and ran a hand through his dark hair. "Business?" he asked.

"Sort of. We're going over to the Palace. It may be there's somebody there I'll want to arrest."

His possum grin came and went. "That'll be something new," he said. "Is the reward too small just to shoot him?"

My demon stirred. I gave some thought to wrapping the barrels of the shotgun around Braden's neck so he could carry it easier, but I was likely to need him before long. That idea didn't make me any happier.

"Come along," I said. "Maybe you'll find some voters to impress."

He pulled on his boots, then cinched his gun belt around his waist. "Who is it we're after?" he asked, combing his hair back again.

"Luke MacNally."

"MacNally? Kin to the big fellow? And to that young lady I saw at your place?"

"Brother."

He looked puzzled, then shrugged. "Your business, I guess. What's he done?"

"Nothing, as far as I know. We're going to see that he doesn't."

Braden stopped in his tracks. "Now wait," he protested. "We get started doing that, we'll have half the town in jail."

He had a point, but I wasn't prepared to argue it. "My business," I reminded him.

"You're the boss."

"Glad you remembered. I'll give you a couple of minutes to get around back before I go inside. If I can, I'll walk right up and take him. If not—"

"I'll be there." Braden broke the shotgun and checked its loads. "I gather you want him alive?"

"No matter what."

Braden snapped the gun closed and nodded. "All right. Good luck."

"Do your job, and I won't need luck. Get going."

Finster was standing at the bar, watching a slow night with one eye while his other dreamed on a better tomorrow. The moment he saw me he tipped his head to point the way. Alone at a table near the back door, Luke MacNally sat against the wall. His hat was pulled down so I couldn't see his eyes, but I saw the pistol that lay beside his right hand. A glass and a mostly empty bottle stood on the table, showing why he hadn't gone back to his friends. I nodded to Finster, blinked my eyes to adjust to the dark, and started Luke's way.

Passing softly between the tables, I ignored the few men there, keeping my eyes on Luke. He might have been asleep for all the mind he paid me. The back door eased open and Braden stepped through, the shotgun cradled across his arm. In about ten seconds we'd have Luke wrapped up like a newborn lamb. I allowed myself a smile, and then everything went to hell at once.

"Why, hello there, Sheriff!"

I hadn't even noticed Seth Crabtree until he sang out from the table almost at my elbow. His cackle was loud enough to call hogs.

"Sure good to see you, Bud. Say, did you know Luke MacNally was back in town?"

At the sound of my name Luke threw his head up, his eyes locking onto me with the look of a treed wildcat. His right hand jerked toward the pistol.

Quicker than I could've told it, my Colt was up and level on his chest, the hammer back and all the future I'd ever have with Johnnie MacNally hanging on the weight of the trigger pull. Braden saved me. He nudged the cold muzzles of his shotgun right against Luke's ear.

"Don't," he said quietly.

Luke hesitated, then gave a little shiver and froze up like a wheel with a dry bearing. Braden's hand shot out to scoop up Luke's gun.

Crabtree laughed again. "What stopped you, Luke?" he taunted. "I guess you ain't heard how tight your little sister's taken up with our sheriff!"

My private demon had slunk away when I hadn't shot Luke, but now he came back laughing. I was tired of Crabtree's nose in my business, tired enough to do something about him. I swiped sideways with my right hand. The barrel of the Colt caught the older man a glancing blow across the temple and rolled him right out of his chair.

"Hey!" Finster yelled. Braden made a move toward me, then remembered Luke and stopped. The other customers scattered out of the way like sheep before a wolf. Crabtree had come up on his knees, his eyes as big as cue balls, looking like he couldn't believe what had happened.

"Bud! There ain't no call fer that. I just—"

He put his hand to his face. It came away red from where the front sight had gashed his forehead. He gaped at the blood with eyes gone even wider, and then damned if he didn't dart a hand inside his coat.

I reached him in one long step and backhanded him sprawling with my left hand. Before he could get up again I had my knee in his rum-soaked gut and my hand locked on his collar. I ground the Colt's muzzle hard against his skinny Adam's apple.

"Are you ready to try it?" I whispered to him. His mouth was working, but he couldn't form the words. "Here, I'll help."

I let go his collar and ripped back the lapel of his coat. His hand came out, clutching a dirty handkerchief. I looked at it, then ran my hand over his coat and shirt. He didn't have a gun. He was still trying to talk, but his lips were trembling too hard and his eyes were like a spooked mustang's, all whites. Before I could move I felt the shattering explosion of Braden's shotgun. Dust and plaster fogged down over Crabtree and me.

"All right, gentlemen," Braden said in a loud, calm voice. "Let's all just stand still. Put your guns away."

I looked around. Some of the customers had started toward me and some were scrambling away. Finster stood like a statue of a saloonkeeper. Luke was twisting on the floor with both hands pressed to his back. Far as I could see, I was the only one with a gun out, so I took Braden's remark sort of personal.

Letting Crabtree scuttle away like a crawfish, I stood up about as slowly as Widow Mabry would have done. Braden wasn't so calm as he sounded. He had the same expression I'd seen the day I'd shot Ed

Willis. "You're a killer," he'd said then. "Right down to the bone." His shotgun wasn't quite pointing at me, but it could've been pretty easily. His finger had all the slack out of the second trigger. My mind calculated how far I'd have to turn to line up the silver pistol and whether he could fire first, and my demon whispered I'd have time. I don't know how long I stood there before I holstered the Colt and walked up to my deputy.

"Get your prisoner," I told him. He faced me a moment longer, then bent to pull Luke up from the floor. "What's wrong with him?"

"Had to hit him," Braden said. He wasn't doing any grinning now. "Things got pretty busy there."

"Take him out."

I followed the two of them, keeping my eye on Crabtree and the others. Most of them had found their way back against the walls. They watched us like we were a funeral procession, all but Crabtree. He'd found his feet and his guts and his voice again.

"You can't act that way, Bud Tilden!" He moved after us at a distance, shaking his fist. "Beating up honest citizens! Threatening people! It ain't right! Long as there's decent folks in Comanche, you won't never be elected sheriff of this county! Never!"

He followed us out to the street, yelling. As we went toward the office he was still standing on the boardwalk in front of Finster's, repeating in his shrill, cracked voice, "It ain't right, I tell you! It ain't right!"

We took Luke straight back to the cells and locked him in. "What's this for?" he demanded through the bars. It was the first thing he'd said.

"Safekeeping until Matthew gets here."

"*You* ain't safe, nor never will be." With Braden's shotgun put away, Luke was getting his whiskey courage back. He was about three parts drunk. "My friends'll get me out, and I'll kill you dead."

I almost laughed. Six months ago I would've been hard put to name a real enemy. Now Luke would have to work his way up through a pretty long line to get his chance at me.

"Your friends are gone, Luke. They rode out."

He bridled. "They wouldn't leave. We swore an oath."

"The law was after them."

He tried to think about that, then gave it up and moved on to the next idea in his head. "What was Crabtree saying about you and Johnnie?" he wanted to know.

"Town talk."

"If you've took advantage of Johnnie, I'll—"

"If you're so damned concerned about Johnnie, why'd you leave her alone around that scum you run with?"

He gave me that treed-wildcat look again, making me think he really would try to kill me if he had the chance. Out front I heard the door open and Braden speaking to someone in a low voice. Then Johnnie MacNally came striding past the iron door toward the cells.

"I told you to wait at the church," I said.

"I did. Now you have him, and I want to talk to him."

She was mad clear through, but not at me this time. I let her pass and went out. Just as I was leaving Luke said, "What the hell have you been up to with Tilden to make folks talk about you in the saloon?" and I heard the sharp crack of Johnnie's palm against his cheek. I closed the door and left him to her.

Braden was waiting for me at the desk. He wasn't holding the shotgun, but it was handy. "What's gotten into you, Tilden?" he demanded. "You'd've killed that man, and he didn't even have a gun. What kind of sheriff—"

I cut him off. "Suppose he'd used Annette's name in that saloon?" I asked. "Then what?"

"He wouldn't . . ." Braden stopped, my demon perching on his shoulder. Then he drew in a deep breath and relaxed. "That's different."

"How?"

"Annette and—she—Annette has agreed to become my wife," he finally got out. "I hadn't meant to tell you yet."

I laughed. "I'll just bet you hadn't."

"There's nothing you can do about it."

"Then why do you keep edging toward that shotgun?"

His face went red and he set his teeth. "Are you saying I'm afraid of you?" he asked.

His voice had gone quiet, like he didn't mean to be pushed much farther. I don't know if I would have pushed him or not, because just then the hinges creaked on the iron door and Johnnie came through, looking at us both with wide and curious eyes.

"I'm going home now, Bud," she said.

I shook my head. "Not a chance. It's late, and Luke's little friends might still be hanging around out there. You'll stay in town tonight." Before she could object I turned back to the deputy. "Watch the prisoner. Be careful about opening the front door unless you know who's there. I'm going to get Miss MacNally situated."

Braden didn't like that, but he took it. "Anything else?" he asked with mock politeness.

"If there is, I'll let you know." Johnnie wasn't going to take my arm, so I took hers. "Lock up behind us."

Johnnie kept her silence until we came off the porch

and turned along the street. Then she asked, "Where are you taking me?"

"You can stay with my folks tonight. They'll be glad to see you. Tomorrow you can start home if you want to."

"All right." She walked a few steps more. "I heard the two of you arguing," she said. "What started it?"

"I wish I knew."

"You do know. It's Annette. She's the one you really want, not me."

I stared at her. "Listen, today I came pretty close to shooting two men because they threatened you. Then I broke the law by arresting Luke because you asked me to. Then I nearly killed my strongest supporter because he mentioned your name. You take a lot of convincing."

"You'd have killed Braden, too. I heard your voice. That wasn't about me. It was about Annette, wasn't it?"

"I don't think so. Not at first, anyway. He's been after me from the start, and Annette's just one of the ways he picked to go about it."

She ignored that. "I thought you'd changed your mind," she said. "But you haven't. It's still her."

"You're wrong about me."

"I don't think so. I guess I can't blame you."

I tried to put my arms around her, but she wouldn't have it. "No. I have to tell you something first," she said. "It's about those two men who were waiting for Luke."

"What?"

"Before you showed up at the line shack, Baxter—he's the dark-haired one—said something about a job at Rising Star."

"What kind of job?"

"I think . . ." Johnnie stopped, started again. "I

think they were talking about robbing the bank," she said in a small voice.

I spun her around to face me. "What?" I shook her, then let her go. "You knew *that* and didn't tell me?"

"They won't do it now. Not after what you did to them."

"What you mean is you don't care if they do it now, since your precious brother is locked up and can't help."

"I do care, Bud." She caught my arm. "Bud, I do! Else I wouldn't have told you."

"All you care about is your brothers. I'll bet you came down to the river the other day just to see I didn't find Luke and the others. You were even ready to—"

"No! I didn't know they were there. Not until I saw Baxter."

"And didn't say anything. You talk about my still wanting Annette. All you want is to keep your kin out of trouble. Looks like I'm a poor second after that."

For just the second time I saw Johnnie close to tears. "No. You're wrong, Bud." She winced when I caught her arm again and drew her along. "What are you going to do?"

"Get you to a safe place," I said. "Then we'll see."

Chapter 19

I DUMPED JOHNNIE on my folks' doorstep, brushing aside their questions about her black eye and leaving her to explain the situation however she wanted to. Then I went back to Hart's to get my horse. Except for Johnnie's roan in the corner stall, the place was empty. Glancing up toward the loft, I thought again about that last time I'd met Annette there. It seemed like years ago. That day I was sick from killing a man and scared of the silver Colt. I'd pushed Annette away—right into Braden's arms, as it turned out—and I'd sworn never to fire at another man in anger.

With Reno saddled, I stood for a second and rubbed my hand over the smooth, cold leather of my holster. I wasn't afraid of the Colt anymore. I felt undressed without it. I'd never fired the pistol at a man, but I'd learned a lot more about killing. Mainly I knew it got easier as you went along, and it didn't seem to have any end.

One thing I hadn't learned was how to stop pushing

people away. I'd done it tonight with Johnnie. I thought of going back to try and square things with her, but the day had been long, the night was getting on, and Rising Star was a four-hour ride. Swinging aboard Reno, I urged him out into the dark.

I passed the church, then the Stanton place. The windows were dark except for a sliver of light that leaked through the shades of Will's room. I imagined him sitting up to work on Braden's old pistol the way I'd fussed over the presentation Colt when I'd first gotten it. Then I left the town behind me and took the fork that led to Rising Star.

Everything I knew said Shirey and Baxter wouldn't go through with their plan, if it was a plan. They were crippled up some, and I'd taken their artillery. It was too wild a gamble for me to call Braden in, even if I'd wanted him along, which I didn't. But there was enough chance they'd show up that I thought I'd better play it.

I crossed the river at the same ford I'd used earlier in the day. My mind wanted to stray to the bend where I'd been so close to Johnnie, but I reined it back hard. If one thing hurt more than another, it was thinking that she'd played up to me just to save Luke's hide. I did my best to shake that thought off as I kicked Reno into a ground-eating canter.

Rising Star might have been a ghost town when I got there, which suited me fine. I had time to pick out a spot on high ground sheltered by a clump of trees. It was good as a deer blind; the bank below me was the salt lick that would draw my game in. I tethered Reno without unsaddling, then curled up in a blanket until daylight.

All in all, it was as dull a time as I ever spent. I woke up and chewed two of Ma's biscuits I'd thought to bring, then checked over my Winchester and waited. The bank opened as usual, did a good, brisk business, and closed for lunch. With the afternoon sun hot on my shoulders I took off Reno's bridle and let him graze, wishing I liked grass myself. When the bank reopened I went back on watch until the shade was pulled and the front doors locked by the president and his whole staff, which numbered two. I stayed another hour. Then, figuring Shirey and Baxter would make enough noise to rouse the whole county if they tried to get through the iron-barred doors and into the vault, I called it a day. The only thing I'd come away with was a good case of chigger bites, while Braden had probably spent the day spreading the word about my being a menace to honest citizens.

All of a sudden I missed Davy Johnson. If he'd been there and still alive, he'd have ribbed me pretty hard.

"Hell of a thing. Denned up like a badger, wasting a fine day by spying on a bank. I thought you was smarter than that, Bud."

I could almost see him, bulky in that big sheepskin coat, leaning on his saddle horn and grinning down at me. Then he looked past me toward the bank the way he'd studied the next campsite that night at the Wells. I remembered Trey Bonner chopping firewood while his partner squatted against a tree with his head across his arms.

I'd shot Bonner, and the other man had jumped up to throw a shot at me. I fired back, hardly noticing him at the time. This time I watched him clutch his ribs and fall back against the oak.

I saw his eyes.

And then everything made sense.

The day I'd shown Braden's letter of recommendation to Brother Winslow, I'd stuck it in my wallet afterward. It was still there. I unfolded it, smoothing it carefully across my knee. Brother Winslow had held it to the light. I stretched it to the afternoon sun, looking for a pattern among the high-flown phrases. Someone had spilled water on it once, then had re-penned the smeared words in a darker ink. With the light behind it, traces of the original writing still showed. Most of the damaged places had been where Stone Braden's name was written.

Back when I'd tried to mend fences with Braden, I had accused him of being down on me from the first time we'd met. "That's right," was his answer. "Since the very first time." But I hadn't understood until now.

In the letter, the original first name hadn't been Stone, nor the last name Braden. The number of letters was the same, and the initials, but that was all. The man who called himself Stone Braden had been born with the name Steve Bonner.

I made it most of the way back to Comanche before moonrise. It might have been eight o'clock when Reno went jumpy on me and shied away from the right side of the road. I felt it, too—somebody in the shadow of the trees. Because Braden was on my mind, I figured it must be him. I turned to clear my draw, knowing he wouldn't give me time to get my rifle.

The Colt was just clearing leather when the shadows moved, drew together, became a big man on horseback. "Easy, Bud," a deep, familiar voice said. "It's Matthew MacNally."

"Matthew!" I let the pistol slide back where it belonged as he rode into the light. "You oughtn't to surprise a man in the dark."

He chuckled. "Same to you," he said. "I heard you behind me on the road. Tracking me, were you?"

"I haven't gotten that brave," I told him. "I didn't

know you were within a hundred miles. When did you get back?"

"Just now. I've not been to the house yet. What puts you on the road tonight?"

I told him about Luke, then about Shirey and Baxter and the rest of it. It seemed a good idea to play down Johnnie's place in the story, especially the part about our swim at the bend, so I did. As I explained things, she had happened onto them at the line shack and learned their plans. Then I'd come along, looking for somebody to deliver Matthew's reward to.

"I thought they were acting disrespectful to her, so I asked them to leave," I finished. "The way I put it, I don't expect them back."

"I'm obliged," Matthew said. He sounded so grateful I was surprised. It was comforting to think I might come out of the last six months with at least one friend.

"Do you want to ride along to town with me and take charge of Luke?" I asked. "I'd sure like to get him out of my jail."

"Tonight?" Matthew considered. "Lord, no. I've been tracking him and that riffraff the best part of a month. He'll keep. Seeing the inside of a jail might do him good. Only thing that surprises me is that you thought to lock him up."

"It was Johnnie's idea."

He threw back his head, and his laugh boomed out like a bear's growl. "She always was smarter than the rest of us," he said. Then he looked at me seriously. "Listen, that Shirey and Baxter aren't any too smart, but they're twice as mean to make up for it. You want to watch your back for a time."

"I'll remember."

"See that you do." He sat there for a moment without speaking, then said, "I could boil up a pot of coffee at the house, if you were minded to share it with me."

"Thanks," I said, and I meant it. His offer meant more to me than I could have told him. I wanted to accept, but I knew Braden was waiting back at the office. It was time to settle accounts with him once and for all. "I'd like to do that, but I have to get back. I'm due for a conference with my deputy."

"Tonight?"

"Sooner the better."

Matthew nodded slowly. "It was him I wanted to talk about over the coffee. I been thinking about him, where I'd seen him before." He stopped and cleared his throat. "Only it wasn't him I'd seen, but some of his kinfolk—an uncle."

"Trey Bonner," I said.

That was about the first time I ever sneaked up on Matthew. "Well, now," he said. "How long have you known that?"

"About two hours."

"If you don't mind my asking, what do you plan to do?"

I grinned without putting much humor in it. "Talk to him," I said.

"Want me to ride along?"

The offer tempted me almost as much as it surprised me. I stopped to think about it, but finally I shook my head.

"Thanks again. He's my problem. I'll tend to him."

I saw the gleam of teeth through Matthew's beard. "That's what I figured. Just bear in mind it never pays to stir up a snake unless you're ready to kill it."

I nodded and reined Reno out into the road. Matthew's voice stopped me.

"Two more things," he said. "First, that reward money. I figure to use that to restock our place, give

Luke something decent to do. Maybe that'll settle him down."

"I hope so."

"Second thing is Johnnie. Has she spoke her mind to you?"

This time he was the one who'd sneaked up on me. I gaped at him, but he was waiting for his answer. "Yes," I said, wondering what he'd think if he knew the circumstances. "She has."

"That's good." He kneed his horse abruptly and started down the road, not a whit concerned about how I might have answered.

"Well?" I called after him.

"She did right," he answered without turning around. "Told her she'd regret it if she didn't speak up. You take care, now."

There was light in Amos Stanton's bedroom when I passed, but the rest of the house was dark, and Braden's buggy wasn't in the drive. That made things easier. I didn't want to fetch him out of the Stanton house, but I wasn't going to wait until morning. One last meeting with Braden, and then I could be finished with killing for a while.

The church was dark, too. It seemed strange how a place can be so important for one day a week and so lifeless the rest of the time. Hart's stable was the same way. For a minute I had the vision Annette might have changed her mind, that she might be lying in the loft just waiting for me.

That's how tired you are, I told myself, to be thinking in the past. Besides, it's not Annette you'd like to find up there.

Reno nickered and rubbed his long face against my shoulder to remind me he was just as beaten out and hungry as I was.

"All right, boy," I whispered. "We'll see about some oats and a rubdown just as soon as I can strike a light."

I led him along the straw-floored hall that wasn't much darker than the bottom of a well. Finally I bumped into a hanging lantern and struck a match to light it. The chimney was warm. In the light from the flaring wick I put Reno into the closest stall. I had just started to unbuckle his bridle when he threw his head up like a feisty colt, his eyes showing mostly white. I tried to hold him, but he gave his neck a shake that threw me aside.

"Steady, Reno! What the hell—"

The rest of what I meant to say was lost in an explosion from one of the stalls toward the back. Blood burst from Reno's wide-stretched neck about where I'd been standing a second before. The horse shuddered all over and pitched sideways. Off balance and surprised, I tried to scramble out of the way. I got clear of the front hooves, but Reno's shoulder smashed me against the heavy timbers of the stall, pinning me in place for whoever was doing the shooting.

A man may know his horse weighs a thousand pounds, but he'll never appreciate what it means until half that bulk lands on him. More alert than I, Reno had seen the gleam of light on the shotgun barrels and tried to give the alarm. It was clear to me that he'd saved my life, though it wouldn't be for long unless I could get at my gun.

Braden! I thought. But his name was Bonner, and he'd finally decided to end his gentleman's game. Maybe he'd guessed I knew the truth, or maybe he was just tired of playing. I had come looking to finish our quarrel, but I hadn't counted on him holding all the cards.

The second shot came from the loft behind me—a rifle by the sound. The bullet ripped through the wood beside my head, raking my cheek with knife-edged splinters. I tried to twist lower in the stall, but Reno's weight held me for what seemed a week while he struggled to breathe. Finally his withers gave way. He fell on his side, his breath foaming out in a final wheeze. I slipped free of his head and crouched as low as I could, holding the Colt ready in my hand.

The man in the loft was moving, trying for a clear shot. I guessed the other one couldn't see me, though the shotgun roared again and buckshot made a sieve of the boards above me. I was behind Reno's body now, protected from that direction while I looked for the man in the loft. What I saw was the muzzle flash of his rifle, and I put three shots right square where it had come from before pain and a sick dizziness told me I was hit. A dark shadow leaned out across the loft rail, broke it, and fell headfirst to the earthen floor. The crunch of bone when he hit made me even sicker, but I wouldn't need to worry about him again.

Still covered behind the horse, I crabbed around to look at my side. A three-inch splinter nearly as big as my little finger had been driven through my shirt and on into the meat below my ribs. I pulled it out. Blood soaked the lower part of my shirt and the wound hurt like the mischief, but I was alive and planning to stay that way. Reloading the Colt, I edged to the door of the stall, snapped two quick shots at where I thought the gunman was, then rolled across the hallway to the shelter of the feed bin. The shotgunner fired too late, his charge blasting a piece out of the wall just as I got clear. I reached around the corner to shoot, and he gave me the other barrel so fast I almost didn't get my hand back.

Somebody about half smart would've waited for

help, but I didn't qualify. Besides, I figured the only two lawmen in town were already inside, so it might be quite a while before anybody else decided to mix in. Most of all, I knew his shotgun was empty and my Colt wasn't.

I came around the back of the feed bin fast. He'd trapped himself in those stalls at the back, so I knew just where to look. When he saw me he was just snapping the shotgun closed on a fresh pair of cartridges. His eyes didn't show the slightest fear or hesitation as he slung the twin muzzles toward me.

My bullet took him through the chest and drove him off balance against the side of the stall. He touched off both barrels into the dirt between us, and I shot him again before he fell.

Blood ran into my eyes, blinding me. I blinked it away and dabbed at my forehead. More blood dripped down my neck from where the splinters had cut me. Probably there wasn't much left of one ear, and my side burned like somebody had seared it with a branding iron, but none of that mattered at the moment. The important thing was what I'd seen just as I fired. The flat, fearless snake's eyes didn't belong to Stone Braden. I had killed Shirey and Baxter, but Braden was still around.

"Nothing's ever finished," I said aloud.

Behind me the lantern sputtered and went out, its fuel gone. I left it. Inside the front door I stopped to rest and mop the blood away again. Then I remembered I'd emptied the Colt, so I leaned against the wall while I punched out the spent hulls and replaced them. Just as I was finishing up somebody came running along the alley beside the stable, knocking over the same sheet of tin I'd hit once before. I edged to the door and peered out.

It was Stone Braden, angling across the street in the

moonlight with the county shotgun in his hands. He was coming on at a dead run, straight into the darkness where I stood. I took a breath, lifted the Colt in both hands, and laid the silver sights on the shine of the deputy's badge at his chest.

"Bonner!" I said.

Chapter 20

THE NAME STOPPED HIM DEAD in the middle of the moonlit street. He gripped his shotgun, casting his head back and forth like a hound that's lost the scent.

"You know," he said.

"Finally."

The barrel of the Colt began to shake, and I rested my hands against the door frame. Somewhere along the streets a horse was coming hard. The sound of its hooves almost hid the singing rattle of a buggy.

The horse and buggy might have been in another world so far as Bonner and I were concerned. He was still trying to find me in the shadows of the door.

"I heard shooting. Are you all right?"

"I'll live."

That struck me as funny, and I laughed. Bonner had been an accomplice in the murder of Davy Johnson. He'd come to Comanche under a false name, planning some new kind of devilment, and he'd even fooled the law into giving him a badge. He had trifled with

Annette, using her as a tool to get to me. And when his killer friends missed me in the stable he had come to finish the job. That's the way it would look, and there wasn't a soul in the county—not even Annette—who could make a case against me for killing him. I grinned in the darkness and drew the hammer back to full cock.

"Who was doing the shooting?"

"Names were Shirey and Baxter. In the same line of work you followed."

Bonner's shoulders slumped a little. "I was in it less than a month. I don't guess that matters to you."

"Not much. Were you that proud of Trey Bonner?"

"I was grateful to be free of him."

My head was spinning. I took one hand off the gun butt to brush at the blood again. Something didn't make sense, something I needed to ask before I killed Bonner.

"Why?" That was it. "You knew he was a killer. You knew it wasn't my doing. Why have you been dogging me all these months?"

He stiffened and brought the shotgun down a little. I steadied my aim. At first I thought he was going to shoot instead of answering, but then he shook his head.

"I left him," he said softly. "You made me run."

Of course. He had acted the coward, and he hated me because of it. He'd left his honor nailed to that tree, and he'd been waiting months for the chance to get it back without getting killed in the process.

"Gentlemen don't run. Is that it?"

"That's it. Not ever again." His voice cracked suddenly. "Damn you, Tilden, quit playing with me! I know you're going to kill me. Do it!"

The buggy rattled around the corner at the top of the street. I didn't look its way. Bonner's advice was the best he would ever give me. It seemed to me that one pull of the Colt's trigger would win back everything he'd stolen from me—my good name, my place in the town, maybe even Annette if I wanted her. I already knew what Matthew MacNally would say: "Just bear in mind it never pays to stir up a snake unless you're ready to kill it."

Trouble was, another face and voice kept getting between the gunsight and Bonner's chest. "You weren't born for a killer, Bud," I could hear Pa saying. "But it's something 'most anybody can learn. Once you pick it up, it's mighty hard to put it down again."

From Trey Bonner up through Shirey and Baxter, I'd had some reason that went beyond me every time I'd shot at a man. Not this time. If I killed Bonner, it would be for personal gain, just like I'd shot him in a holdup. Then probably Will Stanton would come after me with the old black powder revolver, and maybe Amos and Annette and her ma after that. If not them, it would be somebody else, and I could always find a reason for that one more pull of the trigger.

If Pa had been right, if I wasn't a killer, now was the time I'd have to prove it.

I lowered the gun, seated it in its slicked-up holster, and stepped out into the moonlight to face Steve Bonner.

Immediately he brought the shotgun down and laid its ears back. Not until then did I see that he had the same choice. I knew enough to send him to jail or the hangman. If he shot me, he could burn the telltale letter, be elected sheriff, and marry Annette, just like that. The whole town knew about the bad blood between us. Hardly anyone would doubt he'd shot in self-defense, except maybe the people in the buggy that was bearing down on us.

"Your play," I told him. "I'm out of it. If you want to shoot, you'd better do it."

My demon told me I still had time to draw and fire, time to save my life, but I raised my hands to shoulder level and walked toward Bonner.

"Stay back!"

"I don't want you to miss. Nobody's running this time, you nor me either."

From the buggy a man was shouting at us, but he was still in another world from the one Bonner and I had laid out for ourselves. At the last second the horse pulled up short. The buggy slid to a stop so near us it kicked dirt over our boots. Annette Stanton leapt out in a flurry of petticoats and ran to Bonner.

"No, Bud!" she screamed at me. "Don't! Please!"

She threw herself against him, but neither he nor the shotgun gave an inch. He looked at me a moment longer. Then his eyes shifted down to Annette, and he lowered the gun until its barrels pointed at the ground.

At the far side of the buggy Amos Stanton was easing himself out of the buggy, using his long Winchester for a crutch. He shouted something, but I wasn't listening.

"Deputy," I said, "there's two men dead in that stable. I'd appreciate it if you'd arrange to get them over to Perry's." I took the envelope with Stone Braden's name on it and held it out to him. "After that, I expect you'll want to do something with this letter."

He took it like a man in a daze, crumpled it in his hand. He put his arm around Annette. She was crying.

"Thank you, Bud."

The voice was Amos Stanton's. He was hobbling along pretty fast for a man who wasn't supposed ever to walk again.

"You knew all along," I said.

"I did. Stone's not the only man in town using another name. He deserved his chance."

I didn't answer him. I figured he'd done as much as Braden to drive Annette away from me. Maybe he'd even been right, the way I'd been headed. I couldn't blame him. I'd done most of it myself, and now it was over with.

"Braden," I said, "I'm pulling out of the sheriff's race. If you'll do the same, I reckon the job will fall back where it belongs."

I also reckoned a gentleman would have a hell of a time ignoring a challenge like that. Turning away from the bunch of them, I walked toward the office to leave my badge and pick up the rest of my gear.

The office door was locked. Johnnie MacNally was pacing the porch, and she came straight for me when she saw me.

"Bud? Is that—" She stopped when I came into the light and put a hand to her mouth. "You're hurt."

I laughed and fumbled for my keys. "Just about," I said. "I'm through killing."

She stared at me. "All that shooting. Was that you?"

"Some of it was."

"I didn't know. I'd have come—"

"Never mind. You had to tend to Luke."

I went straight on through to the washbasin back by the cells. Looking in the faded mirror, I wasn't surprised she'd had trouble recognizing me. My face looked like it had been flayed, and blood covered just about everything that was still sound. I reached up gingerly and yanked a splinter from my cheek.

"Here, let me do that." Johnnie had followed me. She looked at the damage and frowned. "Some of this needs stitches," she said.

"Let him be!" Luke had come to the front of his cell to glare at me. "You've caused enough talk about yourself and him. Tilden, let me out of here."

I turned to look at him. "Not until . . ." I began, but then I saw his ugly grin, and the little hideout pistol in his hand. "Shirey and Baxter," I said. "I guess they stopped off here first."

"Left me this through the window," he said. He waved the gun. "Open this door."

The muscles of my belly tightened, remembering for me just how much damage one of those slow-moving .41 slugs could do to a man. "Your friends are at Perry's, Luke," I said. "They won't be coming back. Their little trap in the stable didn't go so well."

His eyes widened, then went narrow again. "I'll get you for that, too. We swore an oath." His fingers tightened on the gun butt. "Move!"

"Not tonight, Luke. I'm not sheriff any more."

"Luke!" Johnnie went toward him, would have stepped right between us if he hadn't reached through the bars to shove her back. "Luke, you can't do this."

"Shut up. Take his gun."

"No!"

"Take it or I'll shoot him right now. Then get me the key to this cell."

Johnnie came over to my side and slipped the Colt from my holster. Then she fished in my pocket for the keys and stepped away. It was clear to me why Matthew MacNally had always had better sense than to marry.

"All right. Unlock this door."

Johnnie's head was bent over the Colt. I heard the triple click as she cocked it, and then she lifted the silver gun and pointed it squarely at Luke.

"Put the gun down, Luke," she said. "Outside the bars."

"What?" He looked at her and found himself staring down the black bore of the Colt. "Hey, I'm your brother. You won't shoot *me*."

"Yes, I will."

He looked like she'd kicked him. "For Tilden?" he yelled. "You'd kill your own flesh and kin for *him?*"

"That's right."

"You won't!"

"I'll count three."

They sounded like any brother and sister in the world arguing over some trifle. I wondered how many times they must have had that same quarrel.

"One."

He shifted the gun like he was thinking of turning it on her. I got ready to lunge, thinking I might just reach him through the bars, but then he shook his head like a baffled bull.

"Johnnie!"

"Two."

"Aw, hell, Johnnie." Luke lowered the hammer on his gun and sent it spinning across the floor toward me. "That ain't *right!*" Like a kid who'd lost the argument, he threw himself on the bunk, his face to the wall.

I stared at Johnnie MacNally, noticing for the first time as she returned the Colt to my holster that she'd been home to change into that blue dress I liked so much. Tears glistened in her eyes again.

"You were wrong about me," she said. "Right down to the ground."

She would've turned away, but I caught her and held her, getting straw and blood all over the pretty dress in the process.

"And you about me," I told her. "You get out your sewing needle, and I'll tell you about it."

* * *

Todd Milner took my money without counting it. In return he gave me two receipts and a little square box.

"It's not necessary, Bud. I'll be glad to carry it on credit for you if you'd like."

"Thanks, Todd. It's better like this."

"We're going to elect you sheriff anyway, whether you're on the ballot or not. You wait and see."

I finished hitching Fred to the Antwerp Wheel Works buggy and stood back for a look. Todd was right. With yellow spokes and green stripes and real leather on the seats, it was the best-looking rig west of Fort Worth. I loaded my gear in the back, leaned my new rifle against the seat, and climbed up to take the reins.

"We'll see," I said. "Thanks again."

I flicked the reins, and Fred drew the buggy out into the sunshine smooth as a sled on snow. Finster looked up from sweeping his porch and waved, both eyes for once seeming to focus in the same place. I tipped my hat to Annette and her ma, just coming out of the dressmaker's, then turned Fred toward the railroad tracks and Calvin Hart's big corral. Pulling up at the gate, I unhitched him, ran my hand over the powerful muscles in his neck, then turned him in beside Nell.

"You're making a mistake, Bud," Calvin said to me.

"It's not my first one."

"Here," he said. "I'll give you a hand with that." He took hold of one of the shafts and helped me pull the buggy under his carriage shed. "You're sure, now? I'm glad to take them back, but I'd sooner trust you for the money and let you keep them."

"No. Just keep that buggy safe for me until I can afford another team for it."

"That won't be long. You know how that election's going to go."

"We'll see," I said again. I threw my saddlebags across the rump of my mule and tied them in place, then slipped the rifle into its boot. "See you Sunday, Calvin."

Three or four rigs were drawn up in front of the church. The ladies were readying the sanctuary for the big wedding Sunday. I hoped they were doing a good job. I'd turned down the offer to be best man, figuring that was Will's place, but I planned to make a point of attending. Amos Stanton was on his porch when I went by, the sheriff's star back on his vest. He was still taking it easy, letting his deputy handle things for him until after the election was done.

"Bud!" he called. "Stop and sit a minute."

"Sorry. Stock's waiting." I waved and rode on, not ready to visit just yet. I let the mule find its own pace out of town. Too bad, but the best saddle mule in the county would never compare with Reno. But the day was fine and clear, just showing the first of the summer heat to come, and I enjoyed the ride until I came within sight of my front gate. Then Will Stanton came piling off the porch to run and meet me.

"Hey, Bud!" he yelled. "Somebody left your gate down again, and all the stock's out! Johnnie MacNally said for you to get over to the river right away and help her round them up!"

"Right." I swung the saddlebags down to him and rode on through the gate and up the ridge. Near the bend of the river I found the cows and my mules, quietly cropping MacNally grass. Johnnie's horse was off to one side, unsaddled and grazing.

"Johnnie?" I called.

"Down here!"

Her voice came over the noise of the river. I dismounted and led my mule down toward the bank. Out in the channel I could see the lean, sculptured form of a young woman, white as alabaster through the rippling water.

"Johnnie? Is that you?"

"Well, who did you mistake me for?" she called. She swam toward me, keeping low in the water. "It took you long enough to get here. I'm wrinkled like a prune."

"It doesn't show." I took the box from my pocket. "I was coming to see you anyway. I brought you something."

"Did you?"

Kneeling on the bank, I opened the lid and let the sunlight flash on the little diamond. "Oh," she said, bright as a little girl at the Christmas tree. I couldn't have asked for better.

"If you'll have it."

She looked at me, her eyes dancing. "Oh, I think so." She put out her hand, and I slipped the ring on her finger.

"Milner said it would fit."

"It's perfect. He knows all my sizes."

"I hope to learn them." I sat back. "Come on out and we'll go tell Matthew."

"I'd rather you came in," she said. "Dare you."

It wasn't a time to hesitate. I skinned out of my clothes and started to slide into the water. Johnnie stopped me.

"Bud," she said, and she gestured toward the mule.

I knew what she meant. I reached across to draw the Winchester from its scabbard, laying it on the grassy bank within easy reach. I had determined to stop my part of the killing, but there were men who might not feel the same. As long as my name meant anything to them, there would still be snakes, even in our private garden.

"All right?"

"All right."

"What if somebody comes?"

She grinned at me, a blend of kitten and tomboy and little girl and woman. The promise in her eyes was all woman.

"We'll say we're married," she said.

Sliding into the cool welcome of the river and fitting her body and mouth to mine, I knew I'd probably never unravel all the threads that made up John Catherine MacNally. But I intended to spend a considerable number of years working on it.

P